ROMAN ORGY

ROMAN ORGY

Marcus van Heller

and

MADGE BUFORD

Anonymous

First published in Great Britain in 1987 by
Nexus
338 Ladbroke Grove
London W10 5AH

Reprinted 1989, 1992

Copyright © Nexus Books 1987

ISBN 0 352 32057 5

A catalogue record for this title
is available from the British Library

Printed and bound in Great Britain by
Cox & Wyman Ltd, Reading, Berks

ROMAN ORGY
Marcus van Heller

CHAPTER ONE

The slim fingers of the Egyptian slave girl trembled lightly as she guided the penis of her master, Lucius Crispus, into the bronze urn. She pulled back the skin to make it easier for him. She wanted to look away but she didn't for fear she would make a mistake which might cost her a lashing.

Senator Crispus whose banquet it was, lay drunkenly on his side on the couch and relieved himself noisily into the urn. His hand wavered up and fondled the buttocks of the girl as she bent over her task. The long stola which she wore to indicate she was not just any slave, but the slave of Lucius Crispus, did nothing to hide the sleek bulges of her flesh from his caressing fingers. His long, white member thickened slightly in her hand, but then she had drawn the urn away and was gliding quietly away herself. Lucius Crispus turned his attention wistfully towards his guests.

They numbered a good thirty including the few women which his wife Clodia had insisted on inviting for company. Looking around at them where they chatted animatedly on their couches, stuffing themselves with his best wine, Crispus would not repress a smirk of satisfaction. They were drawn from some of the oldest and best patrician families of Rome and they had all come to the fine house of their fellow senator, he who had started life as a small, ambitious farmer, he who could still hardly believe that he was hob-nobbing socially with the descendants of the aristocrats who had ruled Rome since its earliest days.

It was true that some he had hoped might come had sent their apologies or had simply not turned up. Before the wine had mellowed him, Crispus had suffered agonies at the thought that they might still not consider him to be of the proper clay. But now he didn't give a damn. His guests had enjoyed themselves, he knew. And why not? His wine was of the very best. His slaves, male and female, of the most comely. On the tables from which the guests took their fill were panniers of olives, dormice rolled in honey, a ram's head, crab, lobster, wild pig, truffles, succulent mushrooms, a goose – no table in Rome could have looked better. And as a special treat a boiled calf had been brought in, followed by a slave in hunting clothes.

Crispus peered hazily through the welter of sprawling bodies and what seemed like a solid din of voices until he could make out his wife chatting, calmly, with a group of people on the far side of the heavily draped room.

Clodia was one of the most beautiful women in Rome. Her reputation, unlike that of so many of her time, remained unsullied. Crispus knew he had her to thank for his rise in the world. But then, although

8

her wealth had introduced him to new worlds, it was true that it was his good looks and clever, smooth tongue which had ensnared her. He could feel no gratitude towards her. In fact, now that the settlement was made on him, she could have gone, as far as his emotions were concerned. It was simply that his position and vanity demanded the retention of a beautiful and virtuous woman by his side. He had to admit he'd found her very cold of late.

'Well, Lucius, at the risk of being indiscreet, I say here and now that I've never known a better feast.'

Crispus felt his heart warming, his face flushing with pleasure. This was the sort of confirmation he loved to hear. He twisted awkwardly towards the speaker, who was sitting behind him on the same couch. He had quite forgotten the presence of Tullius Canus.

'Could have been better, could have been better,' he said with hypocritical modesty.

'Well, of course, we've yet to see the dancing girls – but if there were a better feast I'd like to be there.'

'Ah-ha. You liked the dinner? Wait until you see these dancing girls. They're real, full-blooded barbarians from the province of Spain.'

Tullius Canus raised his eyebrows, eyes gleaming with voluptuous anticipation. He reached out a pudgy hand and whisked a few olives from the nearest table.

'Nothing better than a bit of barbarian flesh,' he wheezed with a wink at his nearest companions.

Crispus took another long draught of wine from a silver goblet; a long, satisfied draught. Tullius Canus, one of the most powerful and influential orators in the

Senate, was notorious for his attendance at many of the orgiastic banquets of the city. His appetite was well-known. If he was pleased then there was good reason for the host to be pleased.

Crispus clapped his hands and several more huge vats of wine from the hills of Alba were brought in by his slaves. Goblets were filled and re-filled throughout the room.

'Now for the barbarians,' Crispus whispered to Tullius Canus.

When he clapped his hands a second time most of his guests were too drunk, or too steeped in argument, to pay any attention. The noise of voices and laughter droned on, along with the noise of clinking goblets and the clatter of dishes. But when the Spanish maidens danced into the room, there was an immediate hush. They were completely nude.

The fame of the dancers from Spain had spread to Rome, but few had been seen up to now. It was joked that they so excited the governors of the Spanish provinces that they could not let even one out of their sight.

Crispus had, indeed, had to pull strings to obtain the two specimens now moving under the flushed eyes of the company. And he'd had to pay a stiff price as well.

The two girls weaved sensuous patterns in the central space before the couches and tables. Their long black hair swished around their shoulders and the little ebony castanets with which they clacked out a fast rhythm seemed to add a mysterious lustre to their taut, brown skins.

Watching them, Crispus unconsciously passed his tongue over his lips. Behind him he heard Tullius Canus shift his bulk, wheezing, to get a better view.

The girls were slim, but their breasts were enormous. Their pubic hair had been shaven and their strong, slim thighs ran straight into the soft, brown flesh of their bodies.

'Did you ever see such breasts?' Tullius Canus' voice was soft, almost awed in Crispus' ear. 'I've seen a few on my campaigns. I remember a woman in Gaul on Caesar's last expedition. She was a wild one – and well made too. But these. . . .' Words failed him and his eyes bulged.

Crispus forced his hot eyes from the supple movements of his dancers for a moment to steal a swift glance around the room. Everywhere eyes were riveted on the extraordinary proportions of the Spanish girls. His gaze swept back to them with renewed satisfaction. This was going to make him the talk of aristocratic Rome. And the younger Cato was the only one who would disapprove.

The dancers kept time with each other, clacking their castanets above their heads in gestures which raised their breasts upward, then sweeping their arms down in a windmill action to a level with their hips. Their feet pattered on the marble floor which Crispus had had specially laid for the further glory of his name.

'Beautiful . . . beautiful,' Tullius breathed. And Crispus clamped his thighs eagerly together under his toga on the couch.

The dances became more and more lascivious with

11

each of the girls weaving her hips from side to side, pushing out her breasts with a backward movement of the arms towards the guests. Their skins began to glisten with perspiration, giving a sensual oiliness to their bodies. Their buttocks brushed the food tables as they whirled and the guests, some of them laughing and making lewd gestures, others deadly serious with hot, hard eyes, began to clap in time with the castanets.

Face shining with lust and triumph, Crispus leaned forward on the couch. They were well worth the price, he told himself. It was true he had wavered, even though it was Clodia's money – but now he knew they were well worth the price.

Big, bulbous breasts swaying from side to side, seeming about to swing away from contact with their bodies, the girls bent slowly at the knees until they were half squatting, buttocks a couple of feet from the floor. In that position they began a last wild convulsive dance in which their hips seemed to undulate apart from them, describing incredible circles in the air. With every fifth circling they would plunge their rumps down to within a few inches of the cold marble as if running themselves onto a phallus. Every man in the room wished he could have been lying there on the cool marble beneath those plunging thighs to skewer up inside the warm, soft depths of the brown bodies with each descent they made to the floor.

Breathing was heavy in all parts of the room, faces flushed with wine and desire, bodies moving, shuffling uneasily on the luxurious couches.

Clodia must hate this use being made of her wealth,

Crispus thought with a chuckle, and involuntarily he raised his eyes to where Clodia reclined in one of the far couches. He was surprised to see she was not looking at the dancers at all. Her glance was directed at the darker extremities of the room. There was a curious expression on her face which he could not fathom. He tried to follow her gaze, but all he could see were guests, with slaves waiting on them. Nobody was looking at Clodia.

The Spanish maidens were now making a last tour of the room, hips weaving a sinuous pattern in the hot air. Their castanets had fallen from their fingers and now dangled from their wrists on slender gold chains. Their hands clasped the underside of their breasts and offered the full globes with their lush, ripe nipples to the choking aristocrats of Rome. Their hips thrust forward suggestively, thighs wide apart and offering. A single movement would have taken any man they passed right between those lovely legs which promised such delight. But no man moved to break the voluptuous spell which had been cast.

When the girls disappeared, with a final backside quiver at the eyes which followed them right to one of the entrances to the room, there was a momentary hush. All eyes turned to Crispus and suddenly the room echoed with clapping and wild applause.

'Bravo, bravo,' Tullius Canus chuckled behind Crispus. 'that little spectacle alone is worth any man's place in the Senate.'

'I should bring them back for another dance?' Crispus suggested, his bloodshot eyes warm with delight.

'Ah – no.' Tullius lowered his voice. 'That would be a mistake. Don't overdo it. Bring them out every time you have a dinner and your name will go down through the centuries and be remembered even longer than Sulla's. By Jupiter I can see you ruling political decisions of the Senate with your offers to show the beauty of Spanish flesh.' Tullius broke into a roar of deep, contagious laughter which soon had one side of the room rocking. Taking cover of the din, he bent towards Crispus and whispered:

'Give me but one of your beauties tonight and I'll boost your name as the finest host in Imperial Rome – and give my allegiance in the Senate into the bargain.'

'Done!' Crispus whispered back.

The two men sat grinning at each other for a few seconds until Crispus became aware of the hot tension at his loins.

'Excuse me,' he said and looked around for the Egyptian slave girl.

She was standing with averted eyes close to one of the doors. She took badly to slavery. It was said she had been snatched from the Egyptian court, a girl of noble blood.

Crispus clapped his hands and through the resumed babble of voices and laughter the girl turned her face toward her new master and slid quietly through the couches with the urn clasped in her hand.

'This is a beauty of a different sort,' Tullius said behind him. 'A timid deer. What is she like with a man between her legs?'

'I had cause to give her a lashing soon after her arrival and she squirmed nicely,' Crispus replied. 'But as to how she wriggles with a staff in her body I couldn't say.'

'What!' Tullius' voice was a bellow, which he controlled with difficulty. 'You mean to say you've not yet given her the pleasure of a Roman rod in her cranny – an aristocrat's at that?'

Crispus felt his heart beat in gratitude at his alignment with the aristocracy.

The slave girl reached him and fumbled under his toga, pulling it awry to find him. Yes, it had been an oversight, he admitted to himself. But even now there was something which made him wary of raping his slaves – but perhaps it was the noble blood in the girl. And then he scorned the idea. Was he not, himself, accepted as nobility? Had Tullius not just referred to him as such?

The girl's fingers had found the thick tower of flesh and were delicately performing their unaccustomed task of pulling it into view. It was stiff as a Roman sword.

Trembling, the girl held the great erection over the urn. She had vivid, painful memories of the similar weapons with which she had been violated by two Roman centurions, one after the other. She wanted to run away, but her back still smarted from the whipping she'd received for refusing to perform this function a few days ago. She was very frightened.

The hot flesh moved in her hand, seeming to expand. She held up the urn a little while Crispus and the great pig-like man behind him talked in a language she didn't understand and roved hot, drunken eyes over her. Crispus did not relieve himself

15

and she was forced to stand, bending over, holding his sweating organ in her hand – waiting.

'Difficult to see her under that stola,' Tullius was saying. 'You should dress her in a tunic, Lucius.'

Crispus was looking at the girl, at her huge dark eyes, her small, slightly flattened nose, full, crimson lips and that long dark hair which had been torn out from its neat bun by Roman hands and now cascaded around her shoulders like that of the Spanish dancers.

She was quite small. When she walked towards him he could see the slightly outlined mounds of her breasts under the loose-fitting stola, he could see the lines of her thighs as she moved, and now as she bent sideways before him, he could see where the cloth indented slightly between her buttocks, billowing out on either side, tracing the ovals of her rump. His flesh throbbed in her hand.

'You like her? She's quite a beauty, too, in her way,' he said over his shoulder.

'Well I know, by Jupiter, that I'd have been athwart her by now,' Tullius said, shuffling. 'Why don't you strip her, Lucius, and let's see the quality of your latest slave.'

As the slave girl felt Crispus' hands pulling at her stola she was tempted to resist. But she was completely in his power. She had no recourse to justice. Her mind sank into bewildered submission. Only recently, it was said, a slave had broken his master's favourite vase and half the slave household had been killed and beaten as a punishment.

All those around Crispus' couch drew closer as they saw the slave girl's stola being pulled over her head.

Her calves were slim and shapely as they came into view, her thighs slim and strong and then her hips, with creases in the flesh following the bones, dark hair lightly covered the jut of flesh above her mound. Her buttocks were firm and oval, dimpled and seeming to squirm away from the light which suddenly, rudely revealed them.

Forcing her to bend before him, hearing Tullius' approving clucks and wheezing behind him, Crispus pulled the stola over her head and flung it to the marble floor.

The girl tried to cover her breasts with her hands, but Crispus knocked them away with a threatening gesture and the firm, pointed orbs swayed before the lustful eyes of the company.

'Jupiter, she is a sweet little beauty,' Tullius hissed. 'She must have been at pains to hide that from you.'

Crispus felt a little irked. He felt slightly foolish in the eyes of his guests that he had not taken advantage of the sexual splendours of his new slave before this.

Frightened and bewildered, the girl had risen to her feet and taken Crispus' penis once more to direct it at the urn. Crispus felt it pulsating at her touch. He wriggled slightly on the couch and her hand slipped on the flesh. His face flamed and his heart thumped loudly.

'If you don't ram her now instead of trying to piddle in that pot, I shall beg leave to,' Tullius said hoarsely.

Crispus became aware that the whole company was now watching, amused and lustful. He could see Clodia, too, watching him with expressionless eyes from among the women.

17

'Go on, have her, have her,' Tullius urged, 'and give a lead to your guests. Hospitality demands that you show your guests the way and then offer them like facilities.'

'Go on Lucius – and then pass her over.' The cry was taken up by all near the host.

Crispus was sweating with desire. After all, this sort of thing was not uncommon in the very best houses. It should never be said that he was lacking in one iota of hospitality. . . .

He made an indication to the girl and she began to move her hand gently up and down his staff.

Feeling terribly helpless in her nudity, the girl obeyed her master's instructions, revolting though she found them. The presence of dozens of pairs of eyes all ransacking her nakedness, leering at her body and her actions, filled her with a further undefined terror so that she tried to forget the room, the lewd faces and just concentrate on the gentle massage of the great organ in her hand.

She cringed with fright as she felt Crispus' large hand stroke up her thigh and fondle her buttocks. The touch of his flesh on hers was a physical shock which almost robbed her of breath. His hand was holding her bottom, squeezing it, fingers probing lecherously between her buttocks.

All around loud, coarse voices were talking, with eyes which never left her body. Her knowledge of Latin was increasing with each day that passed but she recognised none of the words which filled the hot air around her.

And now the fat, piggish man was moving off the

couch and Crispus was pulling her towards it to the lustful cheers of his guests.

She lay on her back on the couch with a ring of faces pressing around and glaring down on her and Crispus' hand fumbling over her breasts which jutted helplessly towards the eyes above. He was degrading her; he didn't care what he did in front of these men – and women too. He was sucking on her nipples. He was squeezing the plump flesh of her bosom, tweaking it, pressing it.

And now he was forcing her legs wide and his vile fingers were exposing her sex, revealing it to all the world which seemed to be contained in the circle of obscene, salacious faces above her. Crispus' hands were running, trembling, all over her body. His breath jerked as his fingers squeezed the flesh of her belly and she could feel the stark, hot mass on him on her thigh.

She felt lost in a horror from which no god could save her. All these bawdy faces were evil gods, too powerful for anyone to help her; she was descending into the bowels of the earth. Her breath constricted under her breasts as the rigid flesh of Crispus seared into her. He forced her legs wide, abandoning her channel and his surging, violating member to the gaze of the eyes which seemed to dance and laugh, become pink and green, around them. His mouth descended on hers, sucking it, containing it in his; his hands grasped her waist in a vice, pawed her breasts, slid under her buttocks and strained them to his shaggy belly.

'Oooh, what a punishment! What delight!'

It was the voice of Tullius which penetrated Crispus' ears as he jerked in tight, tingling fury into the violated passage of his slave. Crispus' body, as he bucked on the soft flesh beneath him, was a mass of strains and gaspings. Her body was unworldly delight.

Under him she was moaning. Her eyes were screwed tight with pain. Her slim legs were pressed wide, flat against the couch on either side of him.

Flinging his hips at her crotch, he grasped her slim, warm shoulders, and fixed his mouth like a leech on hers. He forced her lips apart, biting them, and pushed his tongue into her mouth. His hands trembled over the sleek bulges of her breasts, gripped the flesh-covered bones of her hips. He took long, slow strokes deep into her body. He didn't want it to end. It was such delight, delight, on and on.

He could hear the drone of coarse, jocular, lustful remarks around him, but he heard nothing specifically, just an accompaniment of noise to the pressure in his groin. And the pressure was growing and growing, his breath gasping hoarsely and dryly, his whole body shuddering – and then the shuddering was a great furious convulsion of hot, burning liquid fire.

Crispus lay on her, body heaving with effort, heart thumping.

He heard the voice of Tullius Canus:

'Come on Lucius. Don't faint on the job. Move over.'

CHAPTER TWO

Among the many pairs of eyes which had witnessed the using of the Egyptian slave girl by Lucius Crispus, was a pair of cool grey. At the moment they were hard eyes, very hard eyes.

They belonged in a face which any Emperor would have been proud of: a broad, strong face with a square jutting chin, a straight fine mouth and a broad forehead from which the eyes looked deeply out, hard and unafraid. A face which could have made a kingdom into an Empire, a face which was going to lead ten thousand men to their doom. The face of a slave.

It was during the lecherous performance of Lucius Crispus that the slave became aware of Clodia's eyes upon him – as they had so often been upon him of late. As Crispus was urged to greater efforts by the licentious crew of Rome's aristocracy, she finally called his name.

'Spartacus!'

He turned his grey eyes toward her and walked over to her side.

As he walked, the muscles in his calves below the

tunic bulged; long lengths of muscle stirred in his arms. In spite of his height – he was slightly taller than any other man present – his body radiated a potential dynamism. It seemed unlikely that he could be taken off his guard.

He bent towards his mistress and the cloth of his tunic stretched in wrinkles across his shoulders.

Clodia's eyes held his with a look he could not understand as she said quietly:

'I'm tired of this. I'm going to bathe. I shall need you to stand guard over the door.'

She bade goodnight to her women guests who watched her sympathetically as she left. It was very hard on her, her husband acting like this in public, and Clodia such a beautiful woman and not one man noticing her leave. It was a wonder she didn't divorce him – or get herself a lover.

Spartacus strode silently after her, leaving the noise of the banquet behind, through the portico flanking the huge quadrilateral, which in turn enclosed the gardens with their walks and arbours and the baths which Crispus had had specially built to the pattern and proportions of the huge public thermae.

It was not unusual for Spartacus to be asked to accompany his mistress. He was the head of the several hundred slaves which Crispus boasted as his entourage and he occupied a comparatively privileged position. Descended from the Thracian princes, he could boast at least as much culture as his master – which he had to admit was not saying an awful lot – and he knew himself to be more of a man.

But lately, it seemed, Clodia had been singling him

out to be with her in nearly everything she did, everywhere she went. He had become virtually, her personal bodyguard.

Watching her walk before him through the torchlit porticos, Spartacus wondered why she stayed in Crispus' house. It was well known – even among the slaves – that he treated her badly. There was nothing to stop her leaving.

Spartacus' lips tightened as his mind dwelt on Crispus. His master treated nobody well, in fact, except those he considered of superior rank and birth on whom he fawned his attentions or whom he tried desperately to impress – not without success.

Spartacus was aware that Crispus regarded him with a certain reluctant respect, which he felt sometimes bordered on hatred. For a long time he had been at a loss to understand this, but eventually it had dawned on him that, to his master, he represented the threat of enslaved but superior classes who in different circumstances would have thought him nothing but an ignorant upstart. There were many such slaves; cultured Greeks and Egyptians, many of them.

He wondered why Crispus did not put him in the slave market at times, to be rid of him, but then again it had dawned on him that he represented a challenge. If Crispus got rid of him, he would have admitted his inability to dominate, admitted defeat.

Following Clodia into the bath buildings, Spartacus wondered why she should require him to accompany her. Was she afraid one of her guests might wander away from the banquet and try to take liberties with her? – nobody would dare. Was she afraid of her slaves? They wouldn't dare – besides he was a slave. Spartacus became suddenly aware of the intimacy of leaving the bright, noisy company and disappearing through the grounds with his mistress to guard her while she bathed.

'Wait here.'

Clodia left him with this command and disappeared into one of the dressing rooms just inside the building.

Spartacus stared around him in the flickering torch-light. Beyond was a large vaulted hall, its walls of blue and white stone mosaic. The centre of the roof was taken up by a large space in the vaulting through which the sun poured at noon and the stars glittered at night. In the middle of the floor was the great bronze basin of water, water which steamed now from the heat of the hypocausta beneath.

The slaves were never allowed to use these baths, which had separate hours – like the public baths – for men and women. It was still permissible in the public baths for mixed bathing, but it was never seen. No woman cared to sully her reputation. There had been so many scandals in the past.

In the past. . . . How many years had Spartacus been here in Rome, in the great town house of Lucius Crispus? How many years had he listened to the suffering and indignities of the slaves? How many years since he had seen his Thracian hills, those beautiful, free, Thracian hills? How long would it go on? . . .

His thoughts were suddenly stopped dead by the appearance of his mistress. Without a glance at him

24

she ran across the marble floor and disappeared down the stone steps into the warm water of the sunken bronze basin. Spartacus was dumbstruck, a hundred times more so than when he had seen the Spanish maidens dance into the banquet room. Clodia had been quite naked!

He gazed incredulously through the ill-lit gloom of the bathing room. It was so. Through the gloom and the rising vapours he could see her white body floating lazily on the surface of the greenish water. Even now he could make out – how anguishingly vague – the lines of her pale breasts, breaking the surface.

Spartacus' mind wouldn't function for some seconds. This had never been known. A Roman patrician woman undressing before a male slave! He turned and peered back through the gloom of the grounds, half afraid that he might be struck down for the sacrilege of having seen what had been paraded before him.

In that fleeting glimpse he had seen the body of one of the most beautiful women of Rome; a body which he knew many noble Romans would have given a fortune to see. Cold virtue in a beautiful woman always increased desire for her.

How could she have been so indiscreet? Why? She could have slipped on her stola and then bathed in one of the smaller baths out of sight. It was as if she had paraded herself intentionally.

Spartacus stood, undecided, at the entrance to the building. He felt he should withdraw to the grounds just outside, but hesitated to disobey his mistress' explicit command. It seemed further sacrilege to remain where he was, particularly as Clodia was making no effort to escape his view, seemed, in fact, to be parading herself quite unconcernedly.

As he watched her misty outline, she turned on her stomach and floated, face down in the water, her long, unloosened hair streaming over her wet shoulders, rounded tips of buttocks showing like some ghostly half-submerged fish.

Spartacus folded his arms. Under his hands he felt the smooth, tight bulging of his biceps and the feeling reassured him. This was Clodia's fault. He would stay where he was.

From time to time, as he watched her leisurely lolling in the warm water, he saw her raise her head, or simply turn it, towards where he stood in the shadow of the entrance. Perhaps she was afraid he would go and leave her unprotected. Although why he would was unthinkable. To disobey an order!

Reflecting, with the image of her nudity in his head, Spartacus began to remember little incidents of the past few weeks: the way her eyes were so often upon him, the fact she had asked his advice upon some Thracian vase she had considered buying, that once her hand had rested on his arm, as if absently, when she gave him an order. Spartacus reflected on these things and gazed with his cool, grey eyes through the steam at the bronze basin.

Time passed. To Spartacus it seemed an eternity, at any moment of which he expected some guest to stray away from the noise of the banquet which he could no longer hear, and find him standing his lonely guard over the senator's naked wife.

But when at last the silent worry of his thoughts was interrupted, it was such an interruption as to fill his head with an even darker cloud of anxiety.

From the bronze basin, Clodia's cultured voice reached him. There was a trace of nervousness in the usually firm, imperious tones.

'Spartacus. A cloth and my robe are in the dressing room.'

He hesitated a second or two for her to add something, but she lay back in the water, waiting.

His heart was beating a little faster than normal as he went into the dressing room. There on a wooden seat were strewn her clothes. His face flushed as his eyes passed, in the gloom, from her stola to the under tunic, the brassiere which clasped those proud breasts, the loincloth which contained those virtuous hips.

He picked up the woollen napkin and the blue robe made of the still rare silk from the mysterious Orient.

As he strode toward the pool, muscles flexing and unflexing in his powerful legs, he was filled with the foreboding of strange things. This was no ordinary night. This was no ordinary duty he was performing.

He reached the pool's edge and stood looking down into the opaque green waters where Clodia, still unconcernedly, floated. She seemed to ignore him as he gazed down at the parts of her body which showed through the steam.

Spartacus waited, while Clodia paddled. He could see the smooth slope of her white shoulders, the deep

27

cleft of the upper part of her breast. Half lying in the water, she turned her eyes towards him.

Her face was radiant with the pale beauty, the clear-cut lines of a Roman aristocrat. Her hazel eyes were bright with a peculiar fire.

'You dislike your master, Spartacus,' she said. Her voice had regained its old, firm tones.

Spartacus said nothing.

Clodia laughed. One of the few times he'd ever heard her laugh.

'Your silence condemns you. He dislikes you, too.'

She hesitated and still Spartacus said nothing.

'Today he finally admitted defeat. He decided to get rid of you, sell you in the slave market.'

Spartacus stared at her. So at last it had happened. But her next words astonished him.

'He wanted to sell you, but I put my foot down. Because I want to keep you.'

'My lady is kind,' Spartacus said softly.

'No, not kind,' she said, 'just self-indulgent.'

Giving Spartacus no time to ponder her words, she began to raise herself to the marble floor of the baths.

He stared at her, unable to avert his eyes as she came, like a nymph, out of the water. First her breasts stunned his eyes, large, firm and white with the red smudge of nipples a startling contrast to the colour of the skin. And then her belly, flat, smooth, white; and then her abdomen, with the two pink creases in the soft flesh and the black down of hair reaching to a point between her legs; and the long thighs, themselves like marble, supple, cold and beautiful.

28

She stood dripping in front of him. Her eyes were those of the sphinx. His lips opened slightly.

'Rub me down,' she said quietly. 'Have you forgotten yourself?'

The whole of Spartacus' skin all over his body seemed to be pulsating as he bent to his task. Clodia stood quietly watching the bunching of his powerful arm muscles as he wiped the moisture from her arms, her breasts, her belly, her back, her buttocks. Spartacus hesitated. Her buttocks were full, contained firmly in long sweeping lines. His hands trembled as he felt their shape and texture through the woollen napkin.

'Go on,' Clodia's voice commanded from above as he knelt. Her voice sounded firm but there was a hollow undertone as if she were steeling herself. He realised suddenly that she was trembling.

His big hands moved down the backs of her thighs, shaping the almost imperceptible down into a slim arrow. His hand contained the rounded calves in the napkin and he swivelled round and rubbed up her legs in the front.

He was more aware of her trembling. Clodia shifted her legs apart, moving on the balls of her small, bare feet. Spartacus looked up at her. Her lips were parted as she looked down on him. Her eyes pierced his with a look which was command and desire and not without a tremulous undercurrent of fear.

'Go on,' she said softly. There was a tremble in her voice as well as her limbs.

Spartacus hollowed his hands around the napkin and moved them up her leg. Astonishment had now given place to a masculine certainty and strength. There was no doubt in his mind, only a deep, luxurious wonder.

His hands moved up over the knee, soaking the moisture from the skin into the napkin. Through it he could feel the solidity of the thigh. He wanted to touch the thigh without the napkin, but he continued pulling the napkin, like a broken glove, up the leg to where it broadened into its fullness and his eyes were on a level with the crease of flesh between her thighs.

Once more he hesitated.

'Go on.' The voice above him was a controlled Vesuvius.

Spartacus held the napkin in the flat of his right hand. With the other he boldly grasped Clodia's thigh, his finger denting the buttery flesh and with a long, slow movement, he wiped the napkin between her legs, dabbing it into the intimate places of her crotch.

As he felt the soft yielding flesh under the napkin flatten out against the inside of the thighs, Clodia's hand moved uncontrollably down to his head and her fingers grasped his long, fair hair and pressed his face to her lower belly.

Spartacus rose slowly up her body, his lips tracing a path up over her navel, the taut flesh of her ribs, resting on the beautiful pearl hills of her breasts, brushing the rich, hard protrusion of nipples, sucking in the hollow of her shoulder, on up the white, slender neck, until they found her lips and fastened there, his lips on those of Clodia, famed in Rome for her beauty, Clodia whose slim, smooth tongue now forced its way between his lips, between his teeth and snaked in his mouth, the mouth of her slave.

After a moment she drew away from him, trembling violently.

'Give me my robe,' she said. 'We must not be seen here.'

Spartacus put her robe over her trembling shoulders, she pulled it tightly around her and, bidding him follow her, walked quickly away from the baths.

Walking behind her once again, Spartacus was filled with a joy of incredible discovery, an emotional power which was overwhelming. Here he was following her as he had so often followed her before – but now what a difference! Now he knew those breasts which had vaguely excited him before as they pressed through her stola. Breasts which had excited so many men in Rome; breasts so inaccessible and far away. Now he knew that slender back which shaped into the girdle of the robe as she hurried before him, knew those buttocks which were outlined by the clinging silk, those thighs over which the silk hung loosely from its swelling over the rump. Now he understood the looks which Clodia had cast toward him. Now he understood the touch on his arm. Soon she would be his, unbelievably his.

Hurrying before Spartacus, Clodia was aware that his eyes were on the tenion of her buttocks under the robe. She pulled the robe tightly around her to give him a more exciting spectacle.

Now they were going to her room and she would seduce him. It was no sudden decision Clodia had made. It had been developing in her mind for months.

31

She was well aware of Lucius' lack of interest in her. She was no longer terribly interested in him. She had in fact made up her mind at one time to divorce him.

But then she had become suddenly aware of the slave, Spartacus. There was some magnetism in him, some superior strength of character which made her, even now, half afraid of her fascination for him.

She had seen Lucius' recognition of the same quality, had watched the battle Lucius, who could not bear to find himself in competition with a stronger man, had fought with himself. She had watched the indifference of the slave to the attempts of an inferior being to degrade him.

It was a fascination, a very physical fascination, which had kept her in Lucius' house. She would sit and watch Spartacus, his big muscles tensing in his big body as he performed his tasks; she would watch the calm, handsome face and if the cool, grey eyes alighted on her she would look quickly away lest he should notice her interest.

The desire had grown in her to touch that athletic, muscular body. A desire which had finally found its outlet a few days before when she had allowed her fingers to rest lightly on his arm while directing him to some duty.

And then she had wanted that touch, that physical communion returned. Had wanted to give, to yield under the superior power which she sensed in the man.

Even now it was a desire completely physical which drove her on. The unheard of, forbidden liaison with a slave. That taboo which gave such an emotional desperation and glory to the act.

Although, it was true, a slave could eventually become a freedman – and perhaps rise to office – there was no denying the fact that a slave, as a slave, was the scum of the Empire. Such a liaison would have the whole of Rome howling for the blood of both parties; such a liaison would resound beyond the boundaries of the peninsula to the very outposts of the Empire.

It was partly the knowledge of this that had driven Clodia on in her desire rather than deterred her. She had a will the equal of most in the city and Spartacus, all unwittingly, had driven her towards the inevitable with every movement of his body, every look in his eyes, every one of the few words he ever uttered.

The noise of the banquet, still in progress, reached them as they walked in the shadow of the portico and mounted the steps to the upper story. Without a word, Clodia led the way through Crispus' room to her own. Starlight shone in through the window which looked out onto the quadrilateral. Spartacus moved uncertainly in the poor light and stood silent and still, while Clodia pulled a heavy shutter into place across the window. She lit torches in their brackets on the walls, and while she moved quietly to the door to close it, Spartacus looked with quick curiosity around her room, which he was seeing for the first time.

The room was dominated by Clodia's bed, the bed in which she must have spent so many lonely nights, listening perhaps to the breathing of her husband in the next room. It was a huge bed of oak. The wood-

33

work was inlaid with tortoise-shell, the feet were made of ivory. All three materials shone with a lustre which bespoke much labour from Clodia's female slaves. There were two divans also, strewn with exotically coloured cushions, and in a corner near the window space was a tripod table on which lay Clodia's mirrors of silver and a few adornments.

The furniture, as was customary in the grand houses, was sparse but superb.

After Clodia had shut the door she and Spartacus stood looking at each other for a few moments. Her beautiful face was slightly flushed; there was a tint of fear in her eyes which she tried vainly to conceal.

The interval of walking had made Spartacus wary. He was well aware of the penalty for this sort of thing and, although his length of rigidity had itched against his loincloth from the moment he'd seen Clodia run from her dressing room, he now remained where he was, making no move towards her.

Looking at him, Clodia, too, felt the slight embarrassment that the interval had built. She had a sudden, fleeting fear that she might be scorned.

She brushed past Spartacus and stretched out on the counterpane and cushions of the bed.

'My bones ache with all that sitting in the banquet room,' she said, holding his eyes again with her own. 'I want to be massaged.'

Spartacus moved towards her, his sandaled feet rustling lightly on the floor. She saw in his eyes the deep unwavering purposefulness that so many were to see and it filled her with a shuddering anticipation.

'Have you seen the women wrestlers being massaged in the palaestrae?' she asked softly. And as he nodded, she added, slipping from her robe: 'Well I am just one of them waiting for the masseur. Clodia does not exist.'

As his fingers began to move over her body and her breath fluttered in her throat, she thought, 'Perhaps this is the *only* time that Clodia exists.'

Once again her full, beautiful white body was exposed to her slave. But Spartacus, running his hands over the beautiful tapering arms, the slim shoulders, the glossy swelling of her breasts, knew that he was no longer her slave but her master.

His strong fingers kneaded the firm flesh of her belly, drawing it in little ridges, flattening it with his palms. He stroked the sinuous lengths of her thighs, his chest palpitating, an aching pressure under his loincloth.

His hands rifled her body, knowing the virtuous flesh, all the more sensual for its virtuousness. As his fingers moved between her legs she gave a muffled squeal and jerked over onto her stomach, burying her face in a cushion. Her back heaved as his hands caressed her bare bottom. The white skin of the firm mounds was so smooth it seemed glazed. The hips flowed out from her slim waist, full and receptive; her feet twitched and her thighs rubbed convulsively together as his hands made bold love to her.

Spartacus gazed down, from his ascendant and intimate proximity, on the beautiful rounded lines of her body and choked with a desire to flop his hips down on that filled-out cushion of a bottom and nuzzle his loaded cudgel between the warm, downy pressure of her thighs where they joined her buttocks.

He worked in fingers up between the tight challenge of her thighs, with the flesh giving before his hand, running in ripples up to the arch in which the moist lips nestled.

His hand trembled as he reached his goal, trembled as he was about to touch the intimate secret of Clodia, cold, unfathomable Clodia whose beauty was the talk of Rome. And then his hand, unrestricted now by any napkin, ran along the soft flanges of flesh, savouring their warmth, their heat, their moistness of gentle perspiration.

Clodia gave a sharp intake of breath as his fingers explored, and she slid up the bed overcome with desire. His hand followed and this time she lay still, breathing wildly as his fingers parted the lips.

As he caressed the little clitoris she gave a squeal into the cushion and the squeal became a gasp as his fingers plunged up through the elastic brim of flesh into the warm depths of her passage.

'Spartacus . . . Spartacus!'

She uttered his name as if in delirium and rolled onto her back. Her hands seized his arms, digging fiercely into their strands of muscle and pulled him down on her. Her lips pressed onto his, working on them as if she was trying to eat them; her tongue jerked into his mouth, gliding like quicksilver.

Spartacus dropped onto her, her body taking his weight as if she were some complementary part of him, giving in places, resisting in others.

'Spartacus, Spartacus,' her mouth breathed incessantly, as if she had been saying the name to herself for months and it was a relief to say it aloud at last.

He shifted on her, hips grinding on hers, feeling, even through his tunic, the flesh of her belly billowing and swelling under him. The rigidity of his penis hurt him in its confinement.

Her hands moved round his back, arms locking him to her, legs twining with his. Her eyes were closed, mouth open. She seemed more beautiful in her passion than he had ever thought her before.

'Spartacus,' she breathed. 'Don't torment me. You are the master.'

Feverishly, yet with the same sure glint in his eyes, Spartacus raised his hips off her and slithered out of his loincloth. He didn't bother to remove his tunic; it pulled up to his waist. From the foot of the bed his sandals dropped with a thud to the floor.

Her long fingers came down between his thighs and grasped him, making it throb. Then she was stroking his small, tight buttocks, urging them at her and her thighs had opened wide.

Spartacus slithered down her. He wrapped his strong arms around her body – and with a swift, full stroke, he shot into her like a Roman legion cutting through the tangled brushwood of a forest in Gaul.

Clodia gave a strangled gasp as she felt the dull pain of his entry. He seemed to split her in all directions. He was bigger by far than Crispus.

He thrust into her, splitting her farther and farther as his thickening organ coursed up into the core of her body. She wanted him to fill her; she wanted him to make her ache, make her sore, make her cry with

37

the sweet tears of exquisite pain. At last this man, this silent, magnetic man, was hers, was alone with her in the world, his mind focused only on her and the superb satisfaction of her body.

Spartacus, soaring into her with an unleashed ferocity, felt a tingling in every pore of his body where it touched her. His chest against her sleek, bolstering breasts, his belly against hers, his hairy thighs brushing her columns of marble-smoothness – above all his great, uncovered tool, hot and bursting with sensation, moving tightly, excruciatingly into her lower mouth.

He gasped out his breath, crushing his lips over her face, over all those beautiful features.

Writhing under him, moaning her ecstasy, the cold, virtuous Clodia was in a bitch-heat of passion, pulling her thighs back to her breasts, almost to her shoulders even, wriggling her buttocks so that the counterpane crinkled and dampened under the sweating move-ment. Spartacus exulted in his raging lust.

His hand roamed over her skin, holding the flesh which belonged to him, doing what he liked with the beautiful body which all Rome would have given its eyes to see.

Gripping her shoulders, squeezing until the white skin turned red, grasping the breasts as they overflowed from under him, holding the waist, cradling the buttocks in is big palms, feeling them overflow from his fingers, so that his fingers dug into them as if they were soft, silken cushions.

Clodia groaned and panted as his hands reached

under her buttocks, caressing the soft, sensitive skin, moving down to the source of their liaison.

She spread her thighs to the limit, forcing herself to endure the pain which accompanied the ecstasy, moaning with a masochistic pleasure under his rough impalement of her. His crushing, aggressive weight seemed to be forcing her through the bed, which creaked under the furious rhythm of their intercourse. She felt inside her belly, as in her throat, a sort of growing restriction of breath, a bubble of sensation which seemed to grow and grow until she knew she could contain it little longer.

The heavy staff which surged in the wetness of Clodia's channel was the only part of himself that Spartacus could now feel. His knees slipped on the silken counterpane as he moved up to try to shove more of his length into the passage.

Her chin was on his shoulder. He could feel the heat of her normally cold cheek on his own hot flesh. Her mouth was fluttering over his face. His own name, Spartacus, seemed to mix with the animal noises of her moans. She strained toward him as he felt a heat in his belly move down to his loins. She panted and the gasps became a continuous low-pitched moan which suddenly choked off into a staccato spluttering and screaming as she pushed her belly up at him.

She was still groaning as the tide of life-giving fluid swept through Spartacus making him cry out with the unbelievable ecstasy of it, making him want to destroy this beautiful creature whose body he was wildly ravaging, whose hips still squirmed slightly under his, whose cheek was still against his, whose arms clasped his shoulders tightly, whose buttocks still tensed in his hands.

He wanted to destroy, to make this woman completely his. Passion made his head swim, his eyes glaze. But to his astonishment, Clodia suddenly began to struggle under him, scratching at him with her nails so that thin weals of pain stung in his arms.

'Beast, beast!' she cried. Tears were suddenly in her eyes. Spartacus fought down her arms, held them to her sides as her body writhed to escape. Bewildered he recoiled.

It was as he stumbled from the bed, confused and distracted that he heard a gasp from behind him. He whirled around in horror.

In the doorway, a look of shocked disbelief on his face, stood Lucius Crispus.

CHAPTER THREE

After his gratification on the slim, brown body of the Egyptian slave, Crispus had passed her on for the pleasure of the others in his company. Other female slaves had been seized and a general slaking of sexual appetites had begun.

This sort of behaviour was more or less the accepted thing in libertine circles – which, after all, comprised most of the aristocracy – and Crispus was not terribly concerned about the effect his public copulation would have on his wife, Clodia – nor any of the other women. After all, they had all seen a penis before – even if they hadn't seen the nook of an Egyptian girl.

When Crispus looked blearily around the room he was hardly surprised to see that Clodia had left. A few women remained – those whose husbands had not yet given way to the temptation of the helpless flesh ready to do their bidding. But Clodia, sensitive soul – he sneered to himself – had left, doubtless to escape from the bawdy atmosphere.

Anyway, she'd done her bit. She cut a fine figure

amongst the women and the reputation of her virtue was flattering for him.

Crispus straightened his toga and slipped his feet into his sandals. He felt hot and rather weary. He needed a bath to round off the evening.

A glance around the room satisfied him that his guests were well taken care of in everything their appetites might demand. He could safely leave them for half an hour.

Carefully he picked his way through the couches on which patrician masculinity throbbed out its passion in the feminine softness of the slaves. He passed through the door into the gloomy cool night air of the portico with the grounds and the baths beyond.

It was as he strolled noiselessly in the dimness of the portico's columns that he saw the two figures pass and disappear up a stairway into the house. He stood still for a moment in surprise. The first one had been Clodia, the second Spartacus, the slave.

After the minute or two, Crispus walked on towards the baths. For a second he had thought the slave was creeping after his wife, unobserved. But in a moment he dismissed this thought as an absurdity. It was simply that Clodia had been for a walk in the grounds and now she was going to her room, taking Spartacus with her to shut the shutters and ensure that everything was safe. The number of robbers and cut-throats had been growing of late in Rome. One had to be careful – even in one's own home.

Bathing in the warm, soothing waters of the bronze basin, Crispus allowed his mind to dwell on the slave,

Spartacus. He knew he had acted stupidly that day in suggesting that the Thracian should be sold in the slave market. Clodia, quite rightly, had refused anything of the sort. He was one of their best workers and he had a natural power of command over his fellow slaves that Crispus secretly envied. He was afraid that Clodia might have seen through his demand. The idea that he was half afraid of the big slave was one that he hardly admitted to himself.

There was something about the man on which he couldn't quite put his finger. It was hardly any one thing, but a combination of several: his fine physique combined with that strong face – but above all, perhaps, that strange, deep, unafraid look in his eyes. Crispus cursed his own feeling of helplessness when he looked into those eyes.

He climbed out of the bath and towelled himself absently. He'd have to find some way of getting rid of the man eventually. It was too wounding to his self-esteem to have him around.

Crispus walked back through the grounds, pausing to watch the twinkling jets of the fountains. Thinking of Spartacus had made him uneasy.

Back in the banquet room the guests were still eating and drinking. Others were still doing all sorts of things to the slaves and yet others were lolling in drunken stupours.

Standing unobserved in the doorway, Crispus noticed that Clodia had not returned. His eyes searched among the couches and tables. Nor had Spartacus. A feeling of uneasiness continued to grow in him. He told himself not to be a fool, but, nonetheless,

43

he turned sharply and strode along the portico to the stairway leading to the rooms above.

His heart pounded as he mounted. This was ridiculous, he told himself. But they had been gone a long time.

Reaching the door of his room, Crispus heard muffled sounds from Clodia's room. Sounds of gasps and movement. His face blanched. He pushed quickly and clumsily through the darkened room, crashing against a table on his way. As he flung open Clodia's door he heard the words, 'Beast, beast,' spat into the air and an incredible sight met his eyes.

There, pinned down on her bed, struggling, was Clodia, naked. On her was the slave, Spartacus, his great organ still in her, his hips still wedged between her thrown-back thighs. The slave was breathing heavily and in a shattering instant it was clear to Crispus that this scum, this slave, had just achieved the rape of his wife.

He stood stock-still in astonishment and disbelief as Spartacus stumbled from the bed. The slave wheeled around and the next minute his eyes, those cool, grey eyes, which now contained something close to bewilderment, had fastened on him.

In spite of the extra seconds he'd had, Crispus' reaction, due to the wine, perhaps, was much slower than the slave's. He tried to jump aside as the big body lunged towards him, but the great fist caught him on the side of the face, knocking him back through the door and sprawling onto the floor of his own room.

As Spartacus' brawny legs sped past his eyes,

Crispus cried out at the top of his voice: 'Help, help! Slave revolt!'

Clodia had, with her passion spent, her sense returning to normal, heard the sound of Crispus as he knocked over the table in his room. She had understood immediately, with a clarity of mind which was her strength, that she would have to pretend she had been raped.

The alternative was attempted flight with Spartacus, inevitable capture, almost certain death for her, and very certain ostracism from the society which she held dear. The alternative was out of the question.

Likewise, Spartacus had immediately realised her game when he saw her husband standing in the doorway. The stinging weals from her nails impressed on him the fact that he could expect no quarter from the woman who had just joined him in the act of love. The penalty for rape was death. The penalty for a look of insubordination could be death! To flee was the only possibility.

Had it not been for the lecherous capacity of Tullius Canus, Spartacus might well have escaped into the grounds and from there to the dark streets of Rome where he could easily have evaded the pursuit of the night patrols.

But Tullius Canus, who, in an adjoining room, had just enjoyed the exquisite rapture of one of the Spanish maidens, heard the cry of his friend, Crispus, and waddled out into the passage, nudely obese.

The first thing he saw was the slave, Spartacus, whom he'd noticed before, bearing down on him.

45

'What's up?' he began to say when the voice of Crispus rang out from behind Spartacus.

'Stop him, stop him! He's assaulted my wife.'

Tullius Canus took one further look at the big frame which was almost on him, realised he had no time to get out of the way, and flung himself at Spartacus's legs.

The two men crashed to the ground, Tullius clinging to the slave's ankles. Crispus hurled himself on the Thracian's back and fastened his arms around his neck. Both he and Tullius began to call for help.

Spartacus was filled with fury. His considerable strength was augmented from the desperation which knowledge of his fate if taken captive instilled in him. He lashed out with a foot, heard the thud of a hard heel against Tullius' face, felt his ankles immediately released. He pried open the encircling arms of Crispus, staggering to his feet, dragging Crispus with him in the process – and then flung him back on top of Tullius.

He descended the stone steps four at a time – straight into the hands of a group of several guests who had heard the noise of the cries above the dying hubbub of the banquet.

Arms seized him at all levels. He was pulled to the ground, but fought his way to his feet again. One aristocrat's head he split against the stone wall, another he knocked into oblivion with a blow of his fist.

From behind, Crispus and Tullius joined the fracas, dragging him to his knees. Again he got to his feet,

46

using fists, elbows, head, knees, the whole of his body as a weapon.

Despite their numbers, the Romans fell away all around him, slow and clumsy from the night they'd had. Later Crispus was to remember that not one slave of his household came to his aid, and to exact a terrible toll.

Spartacus, breathing heavily from his effort, body running with sweat, saw the patrician ranks draw back, saw his chance to make his escape through their midst when, as if from nowhere, an outer ring of men, broadswords in hand, closed in on him. They were another group of guests, who, at the first cries, had stayed to collect their swords. One of their number had gone out to call the patrols.

Trapped, Spartacus stood where he was, not taking his eyes from the group of men who surrounded him with steel.

'Clodia will say that I raped her,' he said woodenly to the company. 'But it is a lie. She had me watch while she bathed and then invited me to make love to her. How, otherwise, would nobody have heard her cries?'

Spartacus knew as he spoke, that he was simply adding to his crime if that were possible. The fact that he should slander her after raping her would simply add to his infamy in the eyes of the Romans. Nobody would think of believing him.

'What a vile lie!'

The voice, trembling with emotion, was that of Clodia. Spartacus turned and saw her slowly descending the steps as if she had been injured. Her

47

whole being was the picture of violated virtue. He hated her in that moment.

'How could you add so vilely to your wickedness?' She appealed to him, with a voice, that shook, pulling her stola protectively against her. The heart of every man in the portico inflamed against Spartacus with a rage that was half jealousy.

Sword in hand now, Crispus confronted Spartacus. His face was livid with rage and Spartacus wondered why he did not cut him down immediately.

'You scum!' he snarled. 'Death by the sword or the cross is too good for you. I have another way to make you suffer.'

'He should be lashed! Let's lash him!'

The cry was taken up on all sides.

'No, gentlemen,' Crispus' lips drew back from his teeth as he spoke. 'I have an acquaintance who'll make good use of him, an acquaintance who'll give him such a life that he'll never know which day he's going to die. I'll give him to Larcius Priscus for the gladiators' school.'

Crispus had had to think hard. His first inclination had been to have Spartacus tortured and executed. But one could not, even in these days, execute or torture without people knowing about it. And if they knew, they wanted to know why. If it got around that Clodia, his unsullied Clodia, had actually been forced to yield under the ravishing of a slave, her reputation would be torn to tatters and he in turn would feel the weight of the derision of his fellows; his dignity and position would be ruined forever. Only a score of men

48

now remained in his house. He would have to throw himself on their charity.

'How will you enjoy facing death afresh every day?' Crispus snarled, jabbing Spartacus in the chest with the sword. 'Kill or be killed, that's what it'll be and the longer you stay alive the more torment you go through.'

Spartacus' hard, grey eyes held his, and Crispus stepped back a pace. He looked around at the reassuring ring of swords. He was not concerned about Clodia. It was the thought of the reflection of this act on himself that terrified him.

He dropped his voice to a tone which he hoped appealed to the decency in the men around him.

'This has been a terrible blow,' he murmured. 'If the story gets abroad, my wife will suffer agonies of the mind. I trust you gentlemen will find it in your noble characters not to mention the night's events – or at least to ascribe some other crime to this filthy swine.'

'Aye, aye, aye.'

The confirmation came from every mouth.

'You have our word on it,' Tullius Canus said quietly.

His penis dangled lewdly from below his fat belly.

CHAPTER FOUR

It was the day of Spartacus's first fight in the arena.
He had had precious little training. His fellows in
the prison-like barracks, where Larcius Priscus, the
contractor – Death's middleman as the slaves called
him – kept them meagerly, were all slaves, men
condemned to death for crimes, prisoners of war, all
those whose lives were considered to be worth less
than the street dogs.'

Spartacus had talked to some of them in spite of
the strict discipline under which they were kept. The
majority, he found, had committed crimes that only
their masters would consider to be so, others had
been bought straight from the slave market to fill the
programme of butchery on which their new owner
grew rich.

An atmosphere of jocular mournfulness hung over
the gladiators. They accepted their fate, living from
day to day. They knew that sooner or later they would
die.

'Your first fight today?'

Spartacus turned on the rough wooden bench in

the cold, stone dining room and saw Marcellus, the Samnite.

'Yes. For you, too?'

Marcellus nodded. As a Samnite he would fight with the sword and shield. Spartacus, as a Thracian, would battle with the round buckler and the dagger.

Marcellus was in the school because, underfed, he had stolen some of his patrician master's fruit and been caught in the act. He had an athletic build to vie with Spartacus' although he was a head shorter. His eyes were brown and his mouth twisted often into a bitter smile.

'Are you afraid?' Spartacus asked.

'No. I am only sad that my opponent will not be Marcus Sallust, my ex-lord and master.' Marcellus spat on the floor.

'A wish that many here could echo,' Spartacus said.

Later they were divided into pairs. The pairs in which they would fight in the amphitheatre.

When they were marched out through the streets of the town to the arena, Spartacus strode beside a big Gaul who had been given the net and the trident for his protection.

Today's Game was to be a big one with fighting in pairs. The survivors would then be let into the arena two at a time, each conqueror being set upon by another opponent. A sacrifice of some score of men would have taken place before the dusk.

Spartacus and the Gaul did not talk nor look at each other as they marched. Spartacus did not relish the thought of the senseless slaughter, but the instinct to survive was as strong in him as in anyone.

51

Dressed in their chlamys of different colours, all embroidered with gold, the gladiators made an almost gay procession. Only their faces did nothing to add to the gaiety of the scene.

Soon the amphitheatre, its superimposed tiers of stone arcades resplendent in the sun, could be seen by the parade marching to their death through the busy streets of Rome. People gathered at the roadsides to watch the procession pass.

When they were met by valets, who came to carry their arms, and marched through the ground-floor colonnade and one of the arcades which led into the arena, the gladiators really felt the shadow of fear fall on their hearts.

Marching in step on the loose sand which covered the beaten earth of the arena, they heard the hubbub of tens of thousands of people sitting happily on the terraces waiting to watch the carnage which would follow.

The lowest terrace was nearly twenty feet above the arena and inside it and running around the whole circumference of the amphitheatre was the metal grating – also twenty feet high – a grim reminder of the horrors of men fighting beasts.

All over the terrace bets were being laid on known gladiators and as the men reached the end of the shorter axis of the arena and raised their hands in salute to the balustrade-protected terrace of the Consuls, the tens of thousands of voices hushed and the tens of thousands of eyes stared, weighing up the possibilities of the newcomers.

Marched off like animals, the gladiators were

grouped in one of the enclosed arcades at the end of the longer axis of the amphitheatre. It was here they would wait their turn. They could watch the death of their fellows, if they so chose, through a heavy iron grating, which was slammed shut after each man entered the vast expanse to meet his adversary.

Most of the gladiators watched, fascinated, as the first pair came to grips to the accompaniment of the strident tones of a band, and the fever which seized the amphitheatre.

The duel lasted some ten minutes before the first body of the day sprawled into the dust and the first blood mingled with the yellow sand. The victor walked, pale and thankful, to rejoin his fellows; the loser was dragged unceremoniously to another exit by the attendants.

In the arena as the day wore on and the battling shadows of the gladiators became shorter, Spartacus lost interest in the gory, repetitive spectacle. He was aware that Marcellus had won. That simply meant that Marcellus would have to fight again later in the day.

It was sometime after the sun had passed its zenith that Spartacus and the Gaul were let out into the huge oval of ground, alone, and deadly enemies under the eyes of the blood-lusting citizens of Rome.

The terraces, right up to the highest point where the women sat just inside the outermost wall, seemed huge and far away. Spartacus wondered where Crispus was sitting – and if Clodia had come to witness the slaughter which she had created.

He and the Gaul walked out to the centre of the

arena opposite the place of the Consuls and then separated. Neither had spoken a word.

Then, they circled each other. The hint of nervousness Spartacus felt at this strange new entertainment he was providing did not show in his eyes. The Gaul was an old hand.

Spartacus kept on his toes. He knew he had nothing to fear from the trident. It was the net which his adversary held loosely in his left hand that he had to be wary of. The thought of being suddenly ensnared in its coils, jerked off his feet and then helplessly to await his slaughter, sent a cold shiver up the Thracian's spine.

Shouts of impatience came from the crowd.

'Get to it! Kill him! Strike!'

They reached Spartacus with startling clarity and he felt a surge of disgust against the swarms gathered on the terraces to watch and bet on their favourite sport.

And then the big Gaul lunged out with the trident.

Spartacus took the blow on his buckler. The buckler slewed slightly in his hand from the force of the blow and he gripped it more tightly as he backed away and took a second blow.

His dagger seemed small and useless against the long-range weapon of his opponent. He found himself moving around the arena taking blow after blow on his buckler. All the time he watched the burly arm of the Gaul on which the net jerked in a feint from time to time.

The yelling of the crowd had reached a fever pitch, but both men were now oblivious to the din. Sweat stood out on their brows, their muscles were tensed for the other's slightest reaction.

Suddenly the Gaul's net snaked out. Spartacus saw it coming, swayed aside as the trident crashed once more towards his chest to be taken on the buckler. He thanked the gods he'd had a little training at the school.

All the time Spartacus retreated. It was impossible for him to get to grips with his opponent without the risk of being enmeshed in the net.

The noise in the terraces had reached fever pitch. The Gaul was well-known. On his fate depended the wager earnings of a vast portion of the crowd.

Spartacus retreated still, parrying the continual rain of blows. His eyes watched every move his opponent made, but he could see no way of attack.

The close quarters came quite unexpectedly. The Gaul feinted a blow toward Spartacus' chest and with a great deftness of wrist swept the trident down to the ground. Had Spartacus witnessed the Gaul in action before he would have known of the trick he employed.

The side of the trident smashed against his ankle, knocking his feet from under him. He landed on his back, and as the Gaul leapt in, the crowd yelled in a homicidal frenzy.

'Slay! Slay! Slay!'

Spartacus' mind reacted with the cool urgency which came to him in desperate moments.

On the ground, unable to get up, he would tire, inevitably, under the hammer blows of the Gaul. He threw caution to the winds. As the Gaul's sweating face, grim above his black beard, loomed over him, he flung his buckler, with a force which few could have summoned, at the man's legs.

On the verge of victory, the Gaul felt his knees crumple under him as the buckler hit them. He was flung forward on his face and twisted over immediately, whirling his trident round at his opponent in the same movement.

The crowd, delighted at the rapid action, the incredible fluctuation in fortunes of the two gladiators, saw the trident catch Spartacus's arm a heavy, glancing blow as he in turn sprang in for the kill, saw the dagger drop from his hand to the glistening sand.

Down at the ringside terrace, Senator Crispus beamed his satisfaction. Sitting with the women in the outer heights of the amphitheatre, Clodia bit her lips and then glanced guiltily at her companions for fear they should have noticed.

Spartacus' lunge took him with a thud onto the prostrate body. His smarting wrist grasped the trident just above the spot where it was held by the Gaul.

The Gaul's free hand came up to Spartacus' face, fingers reaching for his eyes and the Thracian grasped the wrist as it came.

For several seconds they lay as they were, the slow strain on their muscles the only indication of their struggle.

The eyes of the Gaul were frightened. He was suddenly aware of the greater physical strength of his opponent. He looked into hard, grey eyes and experienced a chill of horror.

On the terraces, the shouting had died. There was a hush; everyone was straining to see.

The trident bent outwards from the Gaul as Spartacus' wrist slowly twisted it away. The Gaul gritted his teeth. His wrist was giving, slowly giving. There was nothing he could do. With his last trick he suddenly let go. The sudden relaxation took Spartacus by surprise. The trident spun out of his hand and thumped to the ground some feet from the two men. The crowd began to scream again.

A desperate relief flashed in the Gaul's eyes. His suddenly freed fist smashed into Spartacus' belly. The Thracian, cursing the folly which had taken victory from him, fell off his opponent, gasping for breath, still clutching at a wrist.

The big body of the Gaul flopped onto him. The hands came to his throat. Above him the face was creased in effort, the teeth bared.

Spartacus caught the man's little fingers and jerked. The fingers cracked and broke and the Gaul cried out with pain. He struggled still as Spartacus twisted from under him, fastening one arm around the man's neck, pinning his arms with the other.

The Gaul's pain-wracked eyes stared up to the clear, blue sky as under him Spartacus tightened the pressure of his arms. The Gaul struggled furiously. It was no good.

Tightening his arm around the man's neck, Spartacus gritted his teeth as he heard the gasps of his adversary.

'Kill or be killed.' That was all there was to it. One could have no pity.

The Gaul choked, heavy upon him. His struggles were weakening. The tens of thousands of voices were yelling. An instructor had come into the arena to make sure there was no pre-arranged trickery between the two gladiators – no relaxing on the winner's part in the hope that a long match would earn a second chance for both men.

Spartacus heard the Gaul wheezing. After a little more tightening, his struggles came to an end. Spartacus continued to squeeze his neck until he saw the sign from the instructor.

He pushed the Gaul's body from him, got to his feet, collected his dagger and his buckler and walked slowly from the arena to the tumultuous cheers of the crowd. He felt slightly sick.

On the terraces Crispus watched the broad back disappear with a malicious glare.

'He'll lose next time,' Tullius Canus said softly, beside him.

Higher up in the terraces, Clodia found her palms were sweating. She felt relief mixed with a strange foreboding as she watched the broad shoulders disappear from the shadow of death into the gladiator's arcade.

There was no repetition during the afternoon of the first time within memory that a man had been strangled to death in the gladiator's arena.

Body after body was dragged from the ampitheatre; the attendants raked and re-raked the sand.

In the gladiator's arcade, Tullius Canus sat beside Marcellus.

'One of each pair comes back,' he said, more to himself than the Samnite. 'One of each pair comes

58

back until later in the day when he'll join his victim. Later in the day or maybe tomorrow or maybe three weeks.'

He looked at Marcellus, whose sad eyes regarded him sympathetically.

'If I were in the Senate, I would stop this slaughter,' he said.

Marcellus smiled sadly.

'If you were in the Senate you'd be betting and getting richer – or maybe you'd be hiring us to perform and add to your prestige.'

He shook his head mournfully. 'It's only those who've actually experienced the suffering and slaughter who'd put a stop to it – and not all of *them*.

From outside the cheers of the crowd heralded yet another death and victory.

'One of us will die later today,' Spartacus mused. 'Inevitably one of us will die. Two men in the prime of body and mind, and inevitably with the chain fight one of us will die.'

Marcellus was silent. He looked at Spartacus and then up at the new victor just returned from the hot arena with the cheers of the crowd still ringing in his ears.

'It does happen.' he said, 'that for a very good fight both men earn their lives.'

'Until the next time,' said Spartacus.

'Who knows.'

'Then if we meet we must fight well – and hope?' Spartacus said with a wry grin.

'Who knows,' Marcellus repeated quietly, his sad brown eyes speculating.

It was more inevitable than it might have appeared that Spartacus and Marcellus should eventually face each other in the grim loneliness of death's arena. They were probably the strongest and most intelligent of the remaining gladiators.

When the chain fight began, in which each victor had a new opponent unleashed upon him of those remaining in the arcade, it was Spartacus who was first to leave the shade for the hot desert of the arena.

Learning all the time with his dagger and his buckler, using his great strength and his cool brain, he survived three fights in a row to the overwhelming enthusiasm of the crowd. Wagers were laid as to how long he would last. He won two more in a row and then Larcius Priscus, fearful lest the Senate should think it a put-up job and lest the crowd should eventually grow impatient with the domination of one man, looked around the remainder of his men and picked Marcellus as the most likely to test the big Thracian and perhaps bring his reign of killing to an end.

When Marcellus was chosen he picked up his long shield and sword and sadly bade farewell to his fellows. There was nothing in his eyes but a resignation to kill or be killed.

Spartacus, waiting in the sun for his next opponent, wondered how long it would go on. Already he felt the first traces of weariness. As he saw Marcellus stride through the iron gateway he felt a curious disgust that he should have to fight this man with whom he'd felt a certain sympathy during the few days past. 'Kill or be killed.' Marcellus, too, was fresh and strong.

The two men began the procedure of circling each other, feet shuffling softly in the sand.

The yells of the crowd wafted over the amphitheatre:

'Don't be frightened of him – he's only killed six today'. . . . 'Slay the superman.'. . . 'Kill!'

Marcellus launched into the attack, cutting at Spartacus with his sword, stabbing at him in the way the Roman legionaries were taught. Everywhere he stabbed, Spartacus' buckler moved as if by magic, always there to take the blow.

Spartacus waited, waited for Marcellus to expend some strength, grasped his short dagger firmly, biding his time.

With Marcellus's first energy fading, Spartacus began to advance, pushing the buckler before him, forcing his opponent to keep cutting at him, to be always on his toes.

Spartacus had, by now, learned to use his buckler as a weapon, and it was as Marcellus made a defensive thrust, that the Thracian sprang in, forcing the Samnite's sword arm up over his head, taking him slightly off balance. His dagger sliced Marcellus's short sleeve and at the same time he dropped his buckler and grasped the sword arm. He had already learned to take only the chances which would allow his short dagger to be an aggressive weapon. At all costs he had to get to close quarters.

Marcellus's shield, also used as a weapon, crashed against his shoulder and then Spartacus' leg had tripped him and they were both struggling on the ground.

Their eyes, gleaming, fighting eyes, met as they struggled.

'If we can make it look good, we'll be granted a draw,' Marcellus said softly.

Spartacus said nothing. Could he trust this man? He recalled the old gladiator's maxim: No quarter for the fallen. His eyes hardened again.

Marcellus too, had dropped his shield, not to be encumbered with its weight now that he was down. His grip was still comparatively fresh and strong on Spartacus's dagger-wrist.

They writhed together, rolling over on the sand. From the terraces the crowds strained once more to try and see.

'In a moment I shall drop my sword as a token of trust.' Once again, Marcellus' lips hardly moved. 'If then you will fall away as I heave, we can recover our shields and start again.'

'What if I prefer not to accept your token?' Spartacus muttered.

'I have nothing to lose,' Marcellus muttered back. 'I covet no titles. I'll take that chance.'

Spartacus did not relax his grip on Marcellus's wrist and as they rolled and struggled, the Samnite's sword suddenly dropped from his hand.

A tumult broke out on the terraces. Those who had bet on Spartacus rubbed their hands and shuffled on their seats for joy.

Spartacus was startled. His grip had not changed. There was no reason why Marcellus should have dropped his sword and put himself in mortal danger. Marcellus's eyes looked into his as their muscles bulged. It was the look of a man who has made a big gamble on another's character and hopes he is not wrong. Spartacus's eyes answered the look.

Violent shouts and urgings were sweeping down from the terraces as Marcellus gave a desperate heave with his hips. It was a strong heave, a heave which might almost have succeeded anyway. Spartacus rolled away, sprawled on the sand and then grabbed for his buckler.

As Marcellus, too, sprang to his feet seizing his sword with one hand and reaching for his shield with the other, Spartacus was on him. If this was to succeed, Spartacus decided, it must look real. He gave Marcellus no time to recover his shield.

Forced back under the advance of the Thracian's shield, Marcellus lashed out wildly with his sword. His eyes were desperate. He had been tricked, they proclaimed.

Again Spartacus swept his sword-arm aside with a blow of his buckler. When his dagger tore a fresh rent in Marcellus' tunic, inflicting a light flesh wound, Marcellus breathed with relief. He realised only too well that Spartacus with his speed could have plunged the dagger into his chest.

They fought on. At one stage Spartacus allowed the sword to catch him a glancing blow on the wirst to send his dagger spinning across the arena and let the blood flow on his arm.

As he parried strenuously, dancing and weaving under the rapid blows of his opponent, he backed to where his dagger lay. Whereupon, Marcellus left him to hurl himself at the spot where his shield had rested,

63

bronze surface shimmering in the sun for a large part of the fight.

Muscles bulged, bodies sweated and bled as the two men fought. The crowd yelled now for one, now for the other and eventually, after the fight had lasted for close on half an hour, began to call for a draw.

Hearing the cries, Spartacus and Marcellus redoubled their activity, slashing and stabbing, advancing, retreating, neither giving the other too obvious an advantage.

The roars of the crowd grew. The men were equally matched, had fought a magnificent duel. Handkerchiefs fluttered on the terraces, the Consuls looked at the public signal, looked at the two men still battling in the arena, consulted each other and waited.

All around the terraces the crowds had risen to their feet, a chant of 'Let them go!' . . . 'Draw – draw!' rumbled around the ampitheatre. The Consuls consulted each other again, brought in a few of the Senate, nodded wisely and raised their hands for silence.

The great crowd hushed and one of the Consuls called out in a clear voice for the men to stop fighting. A draw had been proclaimed, he said. Both men had fought magnificently and would be rewarded with silver plate.

Breathing heavily, bowing before the Consul, the two men in the arena did not exchange a glance.

Next to Tullius Canus, Crispus was furious. 'Silver plate!' he spat, almost in tears.

'He can't last,' Tullius said reassuringly.

64

Up in the summit of the amphitheatre, Clodia touched her lips with a hand which trembled slightly. She was not sure why she trembled.

CHAPTER FIVE

After days of smarting, Lucius Crispus was now pleased with himself. He had paid heavily for another little spectacle which was to take place on the morrow. True, it had cost him dearly, but it was well worth the money.

Tomorrow a certain number of men were to be killed in the arena. Most of them were freshly convicted criminals but a fair sprinkling were gladiators. They were to be killed partly for their crimes, partly for the amusement of the crowds who would again fill the terraces to watch the blood bath. The method would be the usual one in such circumstances – pitting a man clad only in a tunic against an adversary armed to the teeth. After the unarmed man had been – inevitably – slain, his opponent would be disarmed and made to face an adversary as heavily armed as he had been.

Crispus chuckled to himself as he pictured Larcius Priscus standing before him weighing up the advantage to himself of keeping Spartacus as a crowd draw or selling him into the butchery and accepting the considerable sum Crispus was offering him. Few men could withstand the desire for immediate gain – and a gladiator was always a gamble. Crispus made his way to the Senate with a smile of pleasure on his face.

Lying on her couch in her room – the room in which Spartacus had enjoyed her body to the full – Clodia was disturbed. In the first place rumours had somehow spread that something had happened between herself and her former slave, rumours which were ill-defined and uncertain, but nonetheless creating an atmosphere. Secondly, and in a curious way more important, she could not feel at ease as long as Spartacus remained alive.

She recalled how, watching him in the arena, she had simultaneously prayed for his life and his death in a strange prayer which seemed to struggle with itself just as Spartacus struggled with his opponent down there in the sandy enclosure. In another society things might have been different. But Spartacus was a slave and a gladiator; she a Roman patrician. There was no compromise. So she must continue in her listless existence from day to day, wanting him to live, fearing the continuance of his life.

The moment Spartacus had learned of his fate he had begun to plan his escape. From such butchery there was no reprieve. It was a question of 'Kill and be killed' this time.

He had told his plan to Marcellus and the latter, with a band of some thirty, had thrown in his hand with Spartacus.

'We have nothing to lose,' Spartacus had said. With

a wry grin he had added: 'And we have an empire to gain.'

There was little opportunity for planning, but little was needed. Nobody ever thought of a break by the gladiators. Where would they go? How would they live? Many, in fact, preferred to remain and take their chance in the only job they knew and the only one in which they might make a fortune before they lost their lives.

It was just a question of killing the guards.

On the evening that Crispus went home from the Senate, well pleased with himself and looking forward to the bloody day in the amphitheatre tomorrow, Spartacus and his band fell on the guards who watched over their dormitory quarters and then sped silently across the courtyard to the outer gates of the barracks. It was easier than had been expected. They took the gate guards from behind, thrust their daggers deep and left their bodies in the shadow of the inside wall.

Out into the unlit streets of Rome they swarmed, a motley crew in their coloured, gold-embroidered tunics with their strange assembly of weapons. Down the narrow stone-paved streets they sped like ghosts – a soft thudding of sandals, a passing of darker shadows and then silence.

Rome was silent at night. Doors of the dark apartment houses were barricaded against robbers, shutters were drawn, safety chains pulled across the doors of the shops. Occasionally an upstairs shutter would open in a narrow street and a chute of urine would cascade to the stones below. The shutter would close again and fresh silence follow.

All the gladiators had to watch for were the squads of night-watchmen, the armed patrols who, torches in hand, tramped the night streets, cutting the city into sections in their vigilance for housebreakers and footpads.

At the corner of a large square, Spartacus stopped and waited for his companions to reach him.

'We'll head south,' he said, 'out on the Appian Way. There's some wild forest south and we can get food from the farms.'

They continued silently and carefully, flattening themselves in a dark alley to watch one of the patrols pass by, flitting on when it had passed.

It was near the outskirts of the city that a rich man's cortege turned suddenly into the street along which they were running. The torches of the man's slaves lit up the band of gladiators and the man immediately let out a cry for assistance.

His slaves, seeing what appeared to be a large band of armed robbers, immediately drew their swords.

There was little time for thought.

'Join us, friends,' Spartacus called. 'All here are former slaves.'

The slaves hesitated and the approaching gladiators saw there were two women with the rich man.

'They're robbers,' the rich man, a money-lender, bellowed to his slaves. 'They'll slice you to pieces.'

'No they're not, I saw the big one in the arena – they're gladiators,' shouted one of the slaves.

His voice acted as a signal. The moneylender was

69

struck down by one of his slaves and sank groaning to the roadway. Spartacus and his band joined in the ensuing melee, telling the slaves to keep quiet or the patrols would be on them.

The women screamed and were slaughtered, and the whole band – now some fifty strong – raced on through the night, leaving the bodies of their victims sprawled across the street and a crowd of frightened listeners behind the closed shutters of the nearby houses.

By the time the patrols arrived on the scene there was no sign of the gladiators. And when the people opened their doors to see, they found the road was stained with Roman blood.

CHAPTER SIX

By the time the whole of Rome knew of the escape and the atrocities, the following day, the gladiators were far south of the city on the Appian Way.

A hasty meeting of the Senate was convened. A small army was voted to march in pursuit of the fugitives, regrets on the moneylender's family were expressed, security arrangements in gladiator schools were discussed.

In the late afternoon a cohort – some 300–400 soldiers – began the march south beneath the silver eagles.

On hearing the news, Crispus had immediately considered arming all his slaves, immediately reconsidered the wisdom of such action and over all had cursed his folly at not having Spartacus put to death when he'd had him in his power. He then made a special plea to the Consuls, who eventually allowed him a small band of soldiers to guard his house in view of the bad blood between him and Spartacus. They also said there was really no fear of the gladiator's returning to the city and assured Crispus that

71

the whole band would be in chains by the following day.

Walking in the grounds, Clodia glanced uneasily around and drew her stola closer to her shivering body.

During the next day, the band of gladiators grew to well over a hundred. Nearly every Roman villa they passed they raided and released the slaves. Often they had to break heavy chains to free those who had been brought to Rome from far-off lands.

From every villa they took supplies of arms until nearly every man had, if not a sword and shield, at least a couple of spears.

Towns they skirted, leaving the Appian Way and streaming through the inland forests to rejoin the road beyond.

Late in the day a few slaves who had escaped of their own accord, after the news of the gladiators had passed around, came to join them. It was from one of these that Spartacus learned of the cohort bearing down on them in pursuit.

The slave had heard it from his master. His master had said it should have been at least two cohorts as the gladiators were armed and desperate characters. Spartacus nodded. Indeed it should have been two.

The gladiators by-passed Tarracina and marched several miles south to a spot where the hills swept from the Appenines to within a short distance of the road. They were low hills, no more than a thousand feet above the level of the sea. Spartacus considered them ideal for his purpose.

In these woody hills, overlooking the road, he and his men waited for the arrival of the Roman troops.

Titus Philippus leaned forward on his horse, peering along the road in front of him. Behind him his troops marched wearily. He had hoped to catch the gladiators by nightfall. Already the moon had risen in the sky and the sun was sinking below the foothills.

The youngest member of the Senate, he was eager to bring back the gladiators in chains through the streets of Rome. The city had been shocked at the escape, horrified at the slaughter of noble families on the march south. Already the name Spartacus was passing from mouth to mouth in the city. Those who had seen him fight in the arena accepted him as the leader of the fugitive band. Slaves everywhere were becoming restless.

The young commander had been among those to witness Spartacus' skill in the amphitheatre, but to him the notoriety attached to the name was nonsense. Some people would glamourise anything. The man was an ignorant thug, a small blemish on the Roman countryside that should be stamped out immediately.

Titus Philippus did not overtake the gladiators before dusk. He knew they were heading south along the Appian Way; the witnesses had been numerous. He was annoyed that another day would have to be spent on their trail, but his men were tired. He gave the order and camp was made in the shadow of the foothills.

That night he could not sleep. He thought of the patrician families which, even now, might be powerless, reluctant hosts to the gladiators. He had been so sure he would have caught them by tonight. In a sense he felt as if he'd failed. But he'd make up for his slowness. When he caught them he'd have them beaten through the streets of Rome with sticks . . . he'd get the little children to beat them with sticks.

He was still working out refinements of their punishment when the gladiators fell on his camp and annihilated it.

Rome had been stunned by the fate of the troops it had sent in the wake of Spartacus. A handful of the 300–400 men had been the only survivors. Nobody knew whether the gladiators had suffered any casualties, so complete had been the surprise.

The bewilderment had been rapidly followed by rationalisations, explanations – excuses. The number of Roman soldiers had been too few in the beginning; the Senate should have authorised more. The gladiators had doubled their ranks with slaves. They had spies everywhere.

It was decreed that the two Consuls should themselves take the two legions – all that remained, with Pompeius in Spain and Caesar in Gaul – and put a peremptory and salutary end to the gladiators' antics.

While the wheels of organisation slowly turned, Rome went about its business. Nobody was going to be put out by a handful of gladiators somewhere down near Capua.

Last of all to allow himself to appear put out was Lucius Crispus. Since the small band of soldiers allotted to his house had been withdrawn he'd been putting a bold face to the world and tonight he had hired some professional players to perform a play for an invited audience in his house.

The couches for his thirty guests were arranged in a semi-circle at one end of the banquet room, a large space for the players left at the other. A fair section of the aristocracy were present, a fact which pleased Crispus immensely. He looked around for Clodia. She should be here with him to receive the guests. It was very bad form for her to be missing.

Up in her room, Clodia smoothed her hands over the counterpane of her bed. She now knew that something was happening to her. She was not the woman she had been a few months ago. Something was going on inside her head leaving her listless, half afraid, almost dazed. Spartacus was still alive. It seemed that he had some god personally interested in his welfare. She did not think she was being illogical when she believed the odds had been all against him since the day she handed him over to patrician justice. She wished she could separate her conflicting feelings, wished she could decide, once and for all, if she wanted him to die. In some mystic way she felt that her willing him to live would bring it about. If only she could make a decision.

Suddenly she remembered the play, the guests. With a startled lift of her eyebrows she pulled her stola about her and tripped down the steps to the crowded banquet room below.

Away from the public theatres – even there performances were frequently designed almost purely to titillate the audience into an erotic response – productions reached a peak of sensuality.

The tale which unfolded before the fascinated eyes of Crispus and his guests was that of incest and the ravishing of a daughter, who, unlike her sisters, resisted the amorous advances of her father.

'How scandalous!' the patrician woman tittered as realistic movements on a specially provided couch illustrated the ravishing. The actress was a doll-like creature, a mere accompaniment to the actor, who was one of the finest mimes and dancers in Rome.

Men and women in the audience felt themselves grow hot around the loins as the doll-like face assumed expressions of horror, sudden shock, pain and then abasement, as the actor's hips writhed beside her in the acme of suggestiveness. His hips actually jerked against hers in solid contact and it was clear that both achieved a considerable satisfaction from the intimate motion. The actor simulated a panting and the girl opened her mouth and screwed up her eyes in pretended passion.

Crispus' attentive eyes discreetly watched his guests' reactions. Another success. What a pity that business with Spartacus had happened just as he was really creating a name for himself with his lavish entertainment. All around, men and women had bright eyes glued on the actors. What a pity, he thought, that both Consuls had been too tied up with the organisation of the legions to come. Still, everyone else was here with fewer exceptions than at even his banquet.

Clodia sat beside him, looking straight ahead. She

didn't seem to be at all affected by the performance. He wondered if she were even noticing it and for the first time he felt a twinge of pity for her. She was probably still worrying about her rape. It must have been pretty grim for her as well as for him, he supposed. But it was always worse for the man to have something like that happen to his woman.

He looked back at the actors who were just gasping in climax. The auditorium was hushed, savouring every explosion of breath, when a louder commotion suddenly broke out at the back of the room.

Looking around in annoyance, Crispus was astonished to see that the room had suddenly filled with soldiers, fully armed, metal-covered leather tunics glinting in the light of the few torches.

Crispus stood up, others around him turned on their couches, the actors stopped and stared. Crispus was bewildered. What did this mean? Was there some emergency? He was about to call out demanding information when the soldiers who had surrounded the couches stood back to let a tall figure through.

Crispus gazed at the figure, at the face under the burnished helmet of a Roman commander. His stomach turned to ice. He was looking into the hard, smiling eyes of Spartacus.

Beside him, Crispus heard a gasp from Clodia.

'Spartacus!'

At the name a gasp of horror rippled through the room. Everybody seemed to cringe.

Spartacus stood before Crispus, his hand on his sword hilt.

'Did you not expect me back?' he asked in a tone so soft that only those close to him heard the words.

Crispus' mouth opened but no sound came. The room was silent. The gladiators – a chosen score of them – almost unrecognisable in the uniforms of Titus Philippus' former army, were an impenetrable barrier around the room.

'Have you left your voice in the Senate?' Spartacus' tone rose and he took a step towards Crispus, his eyes sweeping over Clodia. 'Have you no words of welcome for the man back from the death to which you condemned him?'

Clodia's mind clouded over as Spartacus' hard, bitter eyes bored into hers. She could hear his voice but she no longer made out the words. There was nothing but his eyes and the memory in them of her betrayal.

A senator moved forward, Claudius Laberius, a bold speaker, who was in the running for next year's Consulship. He seemed to have little understanding of the situation.

'How dare you force your way in here?' he snapped. 'Don't you know, madman, that 10,000 men are preparing in this city to wipe you from the face of the earth?'

He walked close to Spartacus. No slave was going to command his patrician blood. He jutted his face towards the gladiator.

'You'd better get out and fast before – '

Spartacus' hand struck him flat in his face and Claudius Laberius staggered back several places, tripped over a couch and crashed to the floor. When he started, spluttering, to get up, a Roman sword was held at his throat.

Spartacus turned back to Crispus. His eyes looked past him to Clodia. His voice was controlled, almost conversational.

'We were watching the play for a while,' he said. 'We don't want to spoil the entertainment. But we think it would benefit from a change of actors.'

Crispus could not fight down the nervousness in his chest, which betrayed him in a trembling of his lower lips. Spartacus' casualness was all the more ominous.

There was a slight gasp as Spartacus extended his sword and deftly slit Clodia's stola from neck to hem. But nobody moved to her aid. His sword ripped the short sleeves and the garment fell away from her, tumbling against her neighbour.

'Get up,' Spartacus commanded.

Clodia stood up, her body swelling ripely under the thin coverings of brassiere and loincloth. It did not occur to her to disobey. Spartacus' eyes seemed to hypnotise her. Her large, shapely bosom rose and fell. All eyes were on her and Spartacus.

Another delicate slit with his sword and Spartacus had snapped her brassiere supports and torn the loincloth away from her hips. Her breasts, hips and buttocks emerged as if they had oozed from the coverings, splitting them of their own volition. Pale, beautiful and suddenly chilled, she was exhibited to the prying eyes of gladiators and patricians alike.

Crispus was horrified. This was degradation for him. His terror of the ruination of his esteem overcame his fear and he lunged towards Spartacus and gripped

79

the short sleeves of his tunic. Two gladiators stepped quickly towards them, but Spartacus made no move to use his sword. He moved in towards Crispus's body and brought his knee sharply up between the patrician's legs. Crispus groaned, doubled up and sagged to the floor at the Thracian's feet. Nobody moved to help him.

Spartacus looked back at Clodia. She had not looked at Crispus. Her eyes never left his.

The rebel leader swept his sword in an all-embracing movement.

'Choose one from among my men and you and he will act in reality the part of the play we interrupted,' he said.

There was an audible intake of breath all over the room. Looking at Clodia's lovely body, many of the patricians felt, mixed with their fear and disgust, a crumb of gratitude that this ex-slave had allowed them to see what they could never otherwise have hoped to see. Oh to see that voluptuous body, that body which made one's hand itch to hold its breasts, its perfect buttocks, those hips and thighs made to cushion and open under one's weight – oh to see it in any other circumstances!

'Choose!' Spartacus commanded.

Clodia felt numb, her eyes filled with tears which overflowed and coursed quietly down her pale cheeks. There was to be no pity. She saw it in his eyes.

'Kill me,' she said. 'I would rather die.'

Spartacus looked at the gladiators and grinned. They were all staring at Clodia, eyes hot, trying, it seemed, to draw her eyes to them.

80

'See how eager they are.' He turned back to Clodia and the grin was gone. 'Strange you should find them so little to your taste,' he said savagely. 'I remember when you had different desires.'

He leaned slightly forward and traced a line with his sword point from her navel up between her breasts to her neck. His eyes followed the path of the sword and then bored into hers again.

'Choose,' he said with controlled ferocity. 'Or I shall choose for you.'

There was no pity, no mercy. Clodia knew, suddenly, that things were coming to an end. Life for her as a Roman patrician was over. Even if life remained there was the shame, the impossible shame.

'I choose you,' she said softly.

The room had been hushed. But the hush seemed to take on a deeper quality, as if the air itself were stunned into motionless. Spartacus glared at her, surprised and then strangely furious that she should try to ensnare him a second time.

'Marcellus!' he snapped. 'Take her.'

Spartacus watched them take Clodia at sword point to the couch; watched Marcellus, grinning lustfully, strip; saw the rampant penis boom out as they flung Clodia onto the couch; watched her legs pulled apart; noticed the patrician men leaning forward, seeming to forget their danger; watched while Marcellus, unabashed and unembarrassed, crammed into Clodia's still unresponsive body.

Lying under Marcellus, Clodia felt almost no sensation – just a numbed disgust and a dull ache in

81

her vagina where Marcellus bored cruelly into her dry, unawakened passage.

In her degradation, she also felt a deep bitterness that Spartacus had scorned her, had treated her desperate choice as if it were an impertinence. Seeing the end so near she had decided to succumb with this man between her legs – a last clinging to sharp life. But he had scorned her. In front of the noble blood of Rome he had scorned her. And now she had the double shame of the scorn and the unfeeling spectacle she was providing. She closed her eys. The man on top of her was tearing her passage apart with his rough enthusiasm.

The male nobility of Rome could hardly believe their eyes. There on the couch in front of them, the noble, virtuous, beautiful, frigid Clodia was stripped, all her nude charms there under their eyes. That in itself was a sight to make the genitals tingle, the penis lurch from its slumber into a stiff awareness.

But to see her ravaged by a gladiator. That was something from wild dreams, something that would be remembered with awe in Roman history.

Their eyes bulged as Marcellus surged into the spread-eagled body. Her large breasts indented a little under him, her buttocks oozed outward on the couch, her drawn-up thighs were still, resigned.

Marcellus was bending her legs this way and that, raising her buttocks off the couch, leaning up from her for a deeper angle, panting and gasping, Clodia's passage, in spite of her, had lubricated and the entry was less painful for him. He forced her legs obscenely out so that her calves dropped, doll-like, over each side of the couch. Her thighs made the sides of a concave bowl for his hips.

Every man in the room made a mental note that if he – and she – got out of this alive he must do his utmost to possess Clodia during the days of life and strength remaining to him. Every woman felt a mixture of hysteria and hot fascination.

The spectacle did not last very long. Clodia's beauty, combined with her frigidity towards him, had so whetted Marcellus' appetite that he felt himself racing to a climax within a few minutes. He would have liked to stop and draw the whole thing out, but now he couldn't. His long powerful strokes swept up into her inner regions in regular, forcing intrusions. His breath panted in Clodia's face as he fastened his mouth on her cold, horrified lips. He swivelled his small hips in large vigorous grindings. Prostrate under him, suffocated under his weight, her face hot and flushed, her belly filled and hurting, Clodia opened her eyes and saw the scores of eyes feasting on her. In them she saw the thirsting, the lust which would always be there, remembering, when those eyes looked at her. She closed her eyes again. She felt sick and deadened.

With the darkness before her eyes, she felt his strokes grow feverish with speed and intensity. She heard his breath exploding. His lips clasped down on hers and she let her mouth full slackly open against the fury of his efforts. Then she heard him choke. She felt the heat of liquid in her channel, half swooned under his final, brutal thrusts and lay with her eyes closed, sick and unmoving as he stretched his hot, sweating length on the cool softness of her flesh.

Spartacus had watched for a time. Something about Clodia's apathy touched him, made a small dent in the bitter animosity he felt towards her. He remembered how she had responded, led even, in his arms. He had intended to kill her tonight. But now he knew a better way. It would spare her life, but shame her in a way which would remain for her days a reminder of his vengeance. Watching Marcellus panting in passion, Spartacus felt a twinge of pity for the woman. Under different circumstances she would have made a fine woman for him. He felt a slight sickness of regret and walked out into the cool air of the quadrilateral, leaving his men to guard.

Much later, when the streets of Rome were quiet, the house of Lucius Crispus lay in darkness. The off-duty slaves had retired for the night before the play had begun. The remainder now lay trussed up with Crispus' guests in one of the upper rooms.

In another, Clodia lay, hands and ankles bound beside Crispus who was similarly secured. Their faces were lit up by a couple of torches which the gladiators held over them. In the shadow behind the torches Spartacus stood with a branding iron in his hand.

The flames of a torch had flickered over the iron for a long time. Now it glowed redly in the darkness.

'Untie her ankles,' Spartacus commanded.

His men bent and loosened the ropes. She was still naked. Her eyes were filled with a fresh terror. Beside her, a piece of cloth stuffed in his mouth, Crispus closed his eyes, but opened them again as if the closing had not rid him of an image of the scene.

'Pull her legs apart.'

Eager, trembling hands gasped the smooth flesh of her thighs, drawing them wide, exposing the closed portals of her vagina. Spartacus bent towards her with the iron. The light from the torches lined his arms with shadows, enclosing the lengths of muscle as they bulged.

Crispus grunted, trying to raise his voice in horrified protest. Clodia slithered backwards on the floor, cringing from the red glow.

'Hold her.'

Spartacus moved the iron down to her body, ranged it at a point high up on one of her thighs, aimed it at the soft fleshy fullness just before the inside of the thigh joined her crotch.

He looked at Clodia, gagged too.

'This is how a slave is made,' he said. There were evil chuckles from his men in the half-darkness.

With a swift movement, the iron travelled the distance to the white flesh. There was a searing sound, the smell of burning flesh. Clodia writhed under the hands that held her, tore at the gag with her teeth.

When Spartacus stood back there was a little crescent-shaped burn deep in Clodia's thigh. He bent again to the other leg, and Clodia fainted as the branding iron withered her flesh once more.

Spartacus stood up. He looked at the scars with satisfaction. He turned to Crispus with a malicious grin.

'How does it feel to be married to a slave?' he asked.

Later still, there was a soft stirring from the house of Lucius Crispus. The master and the mistress went out into the dark night. She was still naked and she walked in difficulty as if with pain. They were surrounded by the gladiators.

Swiftly, silently, the gladiators hurried them through the stone-paved streets, with scouts going ahead to watch for the night patrols.

They reached the forum without meeting anyone.

A pale crescent of moon cast only a slight, ghostly light over the huge esplanade as Spartacus and the gladiators pulled their prisoners through the portico which was the public entrance to the south side. To left and right a double colonnade of pillars flanked the forum and opposite – more than a hundred yards off through the gloom – the raised buildings of library and law courts made darker shadows.

Spartacus knew the forum well. How often he had passed through it on the way to the market. He knew just where the bronze equestrian statue of Scipio Africanus glinted in the noon sun in the centre of the forum. It was towards this statue of the vanquisher of the great Hannibal that the creeping shadows hurried.

At the base of the statue, rearing above its ten foot high stone pedestal, Spartacus gave a few orders.

Working quietly and efficiently, the gladiators scaled the pedestal, that statue, and hauled Clodia up with them. There on the bronze rump of the horse they lay Clodia on her back, pulled her legs back to her head, spread them wide and tied them round the back of the horse to its bronze tail. Her womanhood and the slave scars on the insides of her thighs were thus presented to the market, to the throngs who would flock into the forum with the rising sun.

From behind the statue, Spartacus surveyed the obscene contortion into which Clodia was tied. In the darkness he could but vaguely make out of the whiteness of her upturned thighs. But in the morning those thighs would be struck by the first rays of the sun.

Thus, one of the most renowned and virtuous women in Rome would smart with shame under the gaze of rude crowds of peasants, under the eyes of the merchants coming to spread their wares, under the warm glances of the lawyers on their way to the courts, the soldiers, strolling senators, slaves brought for sale; the whole of Rome would view the offered intimacies of Clodia, wife of Senator Lucius Crispus. Spartacus smiled with grim satisfaction.

But the work was not yet complete. On Spartacus' command, his men stripped Crispus and flung him bound and gagged, to the ground behind the statue. There he would lie to see his wife's and feel his own shame in the morning. So that he might not roll away to hide from the scene, his ankles were attached to the horse's tail with a long rope. Spartacus knew that Crispus would die a thousand deaths from the ignominy of his plight and Clodia's, he knew that Crispus would carry the stigma of that morning with him to his grave.

Spartacus bent beside Crispus' prostrate body. He saw the man's eyes gleam up at him in the slight moonlight.

'In the morning,' he whispered, 'you will know what it is like to be exhibited in the slave market.'

Before they disappeared into the darkness, Spartacus and his small band left Crispus's purple-banded toga at the feet of Scipio Africanus' horse. They wrapped around it the broken chains of a slave.

In the morning, when the first merchants and the first shoppers found the two naked Romans, they were afraid to touch them in case in some strange way they should be associated with the crime and punished. By the time the authorities had been contacted and one of the Consuls with his cortege of lictors arrived in the forum, the word had spread over Rome and a large portion of the population was crowded into the esplanade, jostling to get a better view of Clodia's charms. Crispus, appealing with his eyes for release, was still tied to the horse's tail.

CHAPTER SEVEN

In the days that followed, while arguments about command and stores kept the legions waiting in Rome, Spartacus and his followers began a large-scale plunder of the countryside to the south of Rome. They appeared unexpectedly here and there, always in the place they were least expected, until even citizens in the northern town of Verona began to feel fear.

Spartacus' numbers grew and grew. More and more slaves flocked to his side. As the country houses were plundered, horses and a certain number of weapons were acquired. Soon Spartacus could muster a rabble army of some thousands. Nobody knew just how many he had under his command.

Behind his horde, a scattered trail of destruction and rape was left. His men were the terror of patrician women. Spartacus was the scourge of the land.

It was a symbolic act of rapine that finally forced the commanders of the legions into a settlement and launched the weight of existing Roman soldiery at the gladiators.

A Senator Catius, who had been a Praetor, a Pro-

Consul in the distant province of Cicilia, had three attractive virgin daughters. Afraid for their safety in the country house he owned on the Campanian plain, he decided to send them to Rome.

Catius was one of the few people rich enough to own a carriage and it was in this, with a strong body-guard of loyal slaves, that he dispatched them north-wards along the Appian Way. He himself accompanied the carriage on horseback.

It was when the carriage was rumbling slowly along the cambered road only a few miles south of Rome and everyone was beginning to breathe with relief, that the little procession was suddenly intercepted by a band of Spartacus' scouts who had been sent north to watch for the departure of the legions.

The slaves fought valiantly, but were no match for wild men now well versed in the art of skirmishing. They were slaughtered and their bodies left in a strag-gling line across the road.

They had, however managed to keep the gladiators at bay while the carriage and Senator Catius made a mad dash towards the capital city. A furious chase began in which the gladiators rode daringly close to Rome before they finally overtook the fleeing carriage.

Catius, twisted on his horse, tried vainly to fight off his enemies as they overtook him, and his daughters shot arrows from the carriage which killed a couple of their pursuers. But their father was cut down and the carriage brought to a standstill when, perhaps, another fifteen minutes of fierce driving would have seen them within sight of the walls of Rome.

There, so near to the Roman legions, the daughters

were pulled from their carriage and mauled, struggling and screaming, to the grassy bank of a roadside tomb. They were rudely stripped and beaten and staked down to the tomb by their wrists and ankles. While a few men watched, the remainder raped the women in turn, satisfying their laughing lust in virgin bellies, while the girls prayed for someone to ride south from Rome, prayed until pain and horror and disbelief filled their minds with a blankness which knew only the suffering of their senses.

After the seed of two dozen gladiators had been sown between their legs, their wrists were slashed and their blood gushed out over their bonds and the tomb of their ancestor. Broken chains were fastened around their necks, gladiators' nets enclosed them and their defiled flesh was stuffed with the great wooden clubs of some of their captors.

Thus they were left, dying on the roadside. Roman nobility was now the slave, bound in chains and nets and rendered sterile by the weapons of the rebels.

Rome, so used to the horrors sown in the wake of the gladiators, shuddered with a fresh chill of horror when the latest outrage was discovered and the legions were immediately marched south without further wrangling. Blood still darkly stained the roadside tomb as it shook to the passing thunder of their feet.

It was on the slopes of Vesuvius that Spartacus strode, organising the barricades, encouraging his men, while the Roman legions marched to battle, helmets dazzling in the sun, the silver eagles proudly raised at their head.

Spartacus was well pleased with his position. Paths up the side of the volcano were few and elsewhere the mountain was so steep that the Romans would only be able to attack slowly and awkwardly. His only fear was a siege — the almost inevitable step for the Romans to take. For that contingency he had a trick in hand.

The gladiator chief's forces had now swollen, incredibly, to almost seven thousand men. To his Roman adversary his numbers were unknown and therein lay his advantage. For behind the barricades on Vesuvius, when the silver eagles fanned out in the valley below, crouched only half that number. The remainder were quietly ensconced on the far slopes of a neighbouring wooded hill. Scouts in the wood would now be watching the legions' flank with keen eyes.

Spartacus joined Marcellus where he stood, higher up than the barricades, looking out over the thousands of Roman helmets and shields, marching and spreading in a solid wall in the valley. On their flank a few hundred horsemen pranced in controlled exhibitionism. At their head rode Consul Gellius who had finally been given sole command of the army by his colleagues. It was a deliberate show of strength. An eagle spreading its beautiful wings before swooping on the lamb. Spartacus grinned down on the might of Rome and seeing him grin Marcellus grinned too. Time would see who was the lamb.

Consul Gellius was slightly irritated as he rode at the head of his troops into the upland valley which Vesuvius dominated. The gladiators had chosen the most suitable spot to resist what he had hoped would have been a short and glorious mopping up of a scourge.

His eyes travelled up the steep, rocky sides of Vesuvius, right up to where he could see the barricades of the enemy – trees and boulders, shields and rubble. It might be that the barricades would crumble under the weight of his troops. Perhaps he could send wave after wave of men one after the other so that eventually some would scramble through the fire from above and swarm into the rebel camp. Anyway, and Gellius gave a grim chuckle at the thought of it, he could easily starve them out if everything else failed. Spartacus had been very foolish to overlook this obvious possibility. Reassured, he turned on his horse and stared back over the tightly packed regiment of his soldiers. The finest army in the world. He smiled at their solid weight of arms, their smart, efficient appearance.

The first assault began soon after the arrival of the Romans in the valley. The Consul wanted the whole business cleared up quickly. It would be an insult to his command if too much time were spent on what, in a military sense at least, was a small matter.

Shields high, swords drawn, the Romans swarmed quickly and solidly up the lower slopes. But as they climbed, the ascent became more and more difficult, slowing them down to half speed. Those on the paths also went slowly, waiting for their fellow-legionaries. Robbed of their usual cover from the archers, they held their shields above their heads as they advanced. But, eventually, even that became difficult as they needed both hands to clutch at shrubs and rocks in order to keep their footing.

Spartacus watched them come through one of the holes in the barricades. Twelve thousand Roman troops lusting for his blood – and here came the first of them. He could see their swords glinting. Occasionally one dropped a spear with the difficulty of the climb and it rolled and clattered down the side of the mountain. He saw the leather of their tunics swaying and flapping with their efforts. Soon he heard their breathing, watched their muscular arms grasping handholds. His grey eyes were cool. He looked along the barricades at his wating men and smiled. Gaining strength from his strength, those who saw him smiled too and turned back to watch Romans struggling towards them.

Spartacus bided his time. What a target. He wondered how they could approach so blindly, so uncovered. Maybe they thought he had only a couple of hundred men and that they would just push away the barricade with their shields and find their adversary cringing at the base of the trees.

Nearer they came, ever nearer. Spartacus waited, stiffening slowly and then, when some of his men were beginning to wonder if he would ever give the command, he uttered a sharp order. A hail of arrows flew down the mountainside, each carefully aimed, each carrying death.

Watching from far below, the Consul saw his first attack fall back. He muttered fiercely to himself as he watched his men crushing to their deaths. The arrows of the gladiators had taken a deadly toll, against which, in such conditions, his legionaries were no match.

As some crashed backwards, clutching their chests, they formed a human avalanche which swept with it those who came behind.

On the paths, after the arrows – less effective as they could be deflected by firmly held shields – the gladiators sent down a shower of boulders.

By the time the survivors reached the level of the valley, Consul Gellius had lost many hundreds of men and the gladiators had not suffered a single casualty.

The Roman commander swore to himself. But it was what he had half expected. He ordered another attack. He was not terribly concerned about the loss of life amongst his ranks. That was what soldiers were for – to lose their lives in the cause of duty. And it would irk him considerably to have to sit down in the valley for a two or three or perhaps even a four day siege.

This time he ordered a regiment of archers to take up positions as best they could behind the advancing legionaries and try to give them as much cover as possible by firing at and over the barricade. He increased the number of men to attack up the paths, ordering them to carry straight on in advance of the others to try to make breaks in the barricade and hold them until those climbing up the rough mountain reached them.

Watching the second attack begin, Spartacus saw clearly the slight variation in strategy. He ordered his men to pile up the reserves of boulders at the paths, thickened his archery defence at these points and prepared to shoot arrows in a high falling mass on the Roman archers, before they dispersed, while they were still thick on the lower slopes.

The first flood of arrows fell short and fire was withheld. Spartacus waited, watching, judging how soon the Roman archers would have to split up to find niches from which to fire up at his men, judging how soon his own archers would be able to reach them. He judged well and the next flood of arrows hit the legionaries, finding them just in range before they began to split and thin their ranks with the awkwardness of the ascent.

But a fair portion of the Roman troops were able to scatter, lodging themselves in crevices, between boulders, any spot where they could fire over the heads of their advancing comrades and be reasonably safe themselves.

Arrows began to fall over the barricades, to search for and find the apertures through which the gladiators were preparing to fire.

Up the paths, the Romans, no more than two abreast, were making rapid progress, sandalled feet scraping on the rock, kicking up little clouds of dust.

Spartacus waited. The Romans were brave enough. They knew just what had happened last time, but still they came on. There was little hope for those in the early ranks. He looked around, along the barriers. His men crouched close to the wall of trees and boulders. The Roman arrows flew too high to trouble them.

Up the paths, as they came, eyes looking ahead at the still barricades, he could see the sweat running on the brows of the legionaries above their shields. He gave a sharp order.

Another rain of arrows hurtled down the paths. As shields were raised in defence, the boulders were released and before many Romans had had time to look, a mass of stone was crashing down on them.

The front ranks were crushed, fell back. Those behind clambered off the paths, clinging to the craggy rocks at the side. When the avalanche had passed they climbed back and tried to rush the last distances which separated them from their goal, but the reserves of rock were awaiting them.

Again a mass of rock bowled down against them, again they clambered to safety – and again. And all the time as the back ranks leapt aside they were picked off with well-aimed arrows. They could get to within a certain point of the barricades, but no farther.

The Roman archers found their volleys ineffective. The trajectory of their arrows was too high in clearing the barricades to fall on the gladiators. Occasionally a clever piece of sniping reaped a reward in the apertures of the barrier, but that happened seldom. Meanwhile the rebels, well ensconced, loosed salvo after salvo of destruction into the legionaries crawling up the rock face.

By the time Consul Gellius called off the second attack his losses were already more than he had expected would be necessary in wiping out the gladiators to a man.

Reluctantly he ordered camp to be made, sentries to be posted. He would starve them from their hill.

Spartacus watched the legions settling with satisfaction. This was just what he had foreseen. He, too, posted sentries and ordered the remainder of his men to rest until nightfall.

It was well after midnight that the small fire glowed from a hill just across the valley from Vesuvius. It gave off a small light, small but important, low down on the slopes out of sight of the Roman camp. The light was seen by one of Spartacus' sentries who made haste to call his leader.

'We have an hour to wait,' Spartacus said to Marcellus. 'Then the way should be clear.'

When, later, the gladiators began to descend in shifts of a few hundred at a time, the little fire had disappeared.

They went carefully, keeping to the paths and moving slowly, feeling their way for loose stones guarding against the slightest noise. On the lower slopes where the descent became easier they came across the first group of Roman sentries, corpses now, throats slit from ear to ear. From the shadow of the trees, Spartacus' own men stepped out to greet him.

'The Roman camp is surrounded,' reported Lucinius, whom Spartacus had left in charge of his forces on the hill. 'All the sentries are dead. We had no trouble. They were watching Vesuvius. We took them completely by surprise.'

'Good,' Spartacus spoke the word like a prophecy. This night was to see the most ignominious defeat the Roman legions had known since the plundering days of the Gauls and the Carthaginians.

In the trees and scrub at the foot of Vesuvius, he waited until all his men had come down from the rim of the volcano. Then he gave a number of quiet orders and they moved out quietly to thicken the ranks of their fellows already surrounding the tents of the legions.

Quietly they closed in, a tighter and tighter ring around the camp. Spartacus came to the very edge of the tents where they stretched away in neat rows in front of him. All was still; the remnants of twelve thousand Romans lying in a sleep from which many of them would never awaken.

Spartacus looked along the crouching ranks of his men as far as he could see them on this side of the camp. He strained his eyes between the tent rows. He could not see his men on the far side of the camp. For a moment he had an unreasonable fear that perhaps they were not there. Ten thousand men was an enormous number to have to kill even if one had the advantage of taking them unawares, in sleep. The eyes of his men were watching him, waiting for an order, motley weapons at the ready. Spartacus hesitated no longer. He gave a sharp cry, the short howl of a wolf. And from all sides his men attacked the tents.

Fewer than two to one were the odds against the gladiators. And many of the rebels had killed three before the alarm was given. The Roman camp was thrown into confusion. Legionaries were murdered in their beds, others cut down before they had time to find their arms; tents collapsed, others were cut down to enmesh the struggling occupants before the slaughter.

Only in the very heart of the camp, the last portion

to be reached, did the Romans have time to realise the emergency, to seize their arms and form themselves into any sort of organisation.

Fighting desperately, with Consul Gellius at their head, losing men all the way, they managed to struggle to their horses. Even then some were hauled down, rider and horse crashing to the ground. But a few, the Consul among them, cut their way through the gladiators and made a desperate flight across the valley, pursued by a host of arrows.

The battle among the tents raged for a comparatively short time. Here and there little pockets of heroic resistance fought a glorious and short-lived action before they were overwhelmed by sheer weight of numbers. No prisoners were taken. For those who had not escaped it was a battle to the death – a battle in which the gladiators were well versed.

When the sun rose over Vesuvius, it lit up a scene of carnage the like of which had been seen on Roman soil only few times in its long history.

With the exhausted arrival of Consul Gellius and the other survivors in Rome, the city was dazed. The unbelievable had happened and Rome was defenceless. The whole of the peninsula was open prey for the gladiator chief and his horde.

In a desperate fear which was close to hysteria, messengers were despatched by land and sea to Pompeius in Spain and Caesar in Gaul.

CHAPTER EIGHT

Losing no time, Spartacus began a march of destruction northwards from Vesuvius. He alone of his men realised the obvious and incredible possibility. He alone saw how near he was to becoming Emperor of Imperial Rome.

Before him stretched the Campanian plain, fertile and welcoming, with its rich little cities afraid and almost unarmed against him.

The first of them, he entered almost without opposition. At first he had considered leaving garrisons of his men behind and pressing on to Rome. But his men wanted plunder and luxury. Having lived their lives in chains they wanted a taste of what had been denied them. Spartacus gave way before their desires and in every town they pillaged and slaughtered, lived on its food, its women, its wine and then left it a burning ruin behind them. All up the peninsula, the perfume of the grapes and the olives was polluted with the heavy tang of smoke from the embers of what had once been towns.

As they moved north up the Appian Way, they

found that greater resistance had been organised against them. Citizens had voluntarily formed themselves into small armies, gates had been barricaded, walls of the cities manned with makeshift weapons.

When they left the road to take Antitum on the coast, they were forced to besiege the city for a couple of days before they eventually broke its resistance.

Once inside the walls, they wreaked havoc as usual and it was while he was gazing with a reminiscent hatred at the amphitheatre that Spartacus thought of another way to avenge his men against the Romans.

A fresh horde of slaves had been released from their chains in the city and these, Spartacus decided, should gain their revenge for their years of servitude and give his men some entertainment at the same time.

Into the arena he had driven a crowd of patrician women clad in their short undertunics. Into the terraces he and his men crowded, forcing with them the husbands and relatives of the women below. Then at a sign from Spartacus, the newly released slaves were let into the arena, naked.

The women, screaming and pleading for mercy, were chased all over the amphitheatre, thrown to the ground and forced to submit to whatever particular pleasure their captor desired. Some women, more attractive than others, were seized by more than one man. Particular rapes became focal points of attraction, according to their strangeness or ferocity, or according to the beauty of the woman involved or the fight she put up.

One such spectacle was the seizing of a woman whose figure, by its provocative proportions under the tunic, gave delight to every man who watched from the arena-slide.

She was chased by three slaves at once and made a great effort to escape them, running blindly towards one of the bolted gates Her tunic curved tautly around her hips as she ran, outlining the sinuous lines of the straining buttocks beneath. Her limbs were long, loose looking and well rounded. Her breasts jutted out from the tunic in sharp, uplifted convexities.

The men took her from behind before she reached the gate and she fell under them. Each one in his lust became almost a lunatic, rubbing his stiff member against any part of her bare skin he could find, feverishly clasping breast and buttocks through the tunic.

The woman twisted and rolled, clawing and kicking. The tunic slithered tightly up and over her bottom leaving it bare and beautiful in the sunlight. Her buttocks grazed against the sand, patches of dust streaking them.

Fighting over her, tearing the tunic, the slaves soon had it off her. The fought over her breasts. One of them had an orgasm during the struggle and fell back on the sand. The other two continued to maul and pummel her, each trying to force himself into the orifice between her legs. Spattered with dust, sand and sweat, the woman fought and fought until eventually they forced her onto her side and took her from either side.

The slave behind her ran his hands over her breasts, holding each, squeezing them, arms clasping her in a suffocating embrace. While the man behind bit her neck in his passion, bringing out little pink scars in her skin, the one performing the frontal attack put his tongue in her mouth and sucked the flood of tears from her tormented, lovely face.

All over the arena similar scenes of carnality were proceeding. The noblewomen were undergoing every kind of ravishment. All were filled with shame and degradation as they lay helpless, after the depravity which had been unleashed on them, in crumpled heaps of bare limbs and breasts.

News of this ignominy was the final bitter pill which pushed Rome into fresh and furious action. It was one of the richest men in the Empire, the banker Marcus Crassus, who financed the rebuilding of the legions. From his own pocket he offered to equip a new army of which he would retain command.

Rome, the Senate, agreed from desperation and in some gratitude although they doubted the motives of Marcus Crassus. His love of power, which, so far, had shown itself only in the acquisition of his great wealth, was well known.

Marcus Crassus began immediately, methodically, and efficiently to set about his task. He had the advantage of the time the gladiator horde wasted in every city they took on their march towards Rome. Everybody knew that had the gladiators besieged Rome straight after their victory they would have taken it in a matter of days. Now it might be too late.

It was while he was bent on his organisation that Marcus received Clodia Crispus into his house.

Since the day all Rome had seen her in the flesh, Clodia had hardly appeared in public. She had begun to divorce Crispus – which pleased him as he would never have been able to live in connection with her since such shame had been endured by him; apart from that she had stayed scheming in her own part of their house.

The degradation through which she had been forced weighed on her like a fever. During the day she went through fresh agonies of mind as she failed to keep her thoughts from picturing the obscene spectacle she had made that morning. At night she wept hot tears in her hatred for Spartacus who had done it to her.

As news of his latest victories and revenge on the Roman aristocracy filtered through to her, she developed an obsession for vengeance.

On her thighs the scars no longer burned, but they had left a permanent mark to remind her that Spartacus had branded her a slave. She would lie on her bed and stare at the marks until tears blinded her and she clawed at the counterpane in rage. She could not live unless she revenged herself on her former slave.

Marcus Crassus looked up with interest and hurried to meet Clodia as she arrived. He knew of her beauty and it was a source of envy to him that he had missed the spectacle she had provided on both occasions.

He had excused himself from Crispus' play performance and he had not had reason to go to the forum early on the following day. The desire-provoking beauty he had thus missed had been relayed to him together with rumours that Clodia had been having an affair with the handsome Thracian and he had revenged himself for her betrayal. Of course nobody knew the truth of these rumours and Crassus took them with a pinch of salt – without of course discarding their possibility – but that Clodia's renowned beauty had been twice paraded before Rome and that on one occasion she had provided half the spectacle in the sexual act were facts which brooked no denial.

'It is a pleasure to see you,' he purred, leading the way into an inner room. She should not think that she had suffered any stigma in his eyes due to her misfortunes.

Settled in his inner sanctuary, to which he had wine and sweetmeats brought, Crassus regarded her while they exchanged pleasantries.

Yes, she was beautiful all right. Her breasts pushed her stola out at a sharp angle so that it pulled in a long slope down to her girdle. He found it difficult to take his eyes off the tilt of her breasts.

She seemed rather nervous – not surprising after her experience – but was at pains to disguise it. In spite of her nervousness, he read in her eyes a look which bode ill for somebody.

Even small talk these days ended on Spartacus and his gladiators. When Marcus Crassus remarked that he'd been rather busy lately fitting out his army and that it was coming along very well, Clodia looked him in the eyes and said: 'It was that which I came to talk to you about.'

Crassus raised his eyebrows in surprise.

'You've no doubt heard of the way I was treated by this beast,' Clodia said, and giving no time for confirmation, continued: 'You must also realise that

106

he's ruined my life in Rome. People do not act towards me in the same way they used to. I'm some sort of circus.'

'My dear lady – ' Crassus began. Clodia cut him short.

'Thank you. But I'm afraid it's true. And I am no longer the same person. There is something which occupies me exclusively.' She paused and Crassus wondered if he should prompt her, decided against it.

'What I want – in fact the only thing I want – is revenge.'

She spat the last words in such a bitter tone that Crassus was startled. He wondered if she was like that when she made love. His eyes lowered to her breasts and fluttered guiltily away.

'I have thought about it a lot,' Clodia went on relentlessly, 'and the best way I can get revenge seems to be to help your army and you.'

Crassus stared at her with a new interest.

'I have no idea what your plans are in a military sense,' she continued. 'But everybody realises by now that Spartacus is a redoubtable enemy.'

Crassus noticed that as she pronounced the name she seemed to hesitate and her lip quivered. He waited for her to go on talking. She obviously had something worked out.

Clodia's eyes still held his as she said: 'You no doubt have also heard that I was branded with the marks of a slave. I may never be rid of those marks so it seems I might as well put them to some use.' She paused. Crassus continued to regard her attentively.

'I believe the battle in which he routed the legions,' she went on, 'was won because of a ruse.'

'That is so,' Crassus said.

'Had there been a spy in his camp – someone who knew what the movements were going to be – I think Gellius need never have fallen into the trap.'

'Very possibly.'

'So all Rome needs is a spy – and I am willing to fill that role.'

Crassus was taken aback.

'My dear lady, that is no job for – '

'I need my revenge,' Clodia cut in fiercely. 'This is the only thing I want to do – to see this man and his ruffians crushed.'

'But for a noblewoman like yourself to attempt such a task would be suicide,' Crassus said. 'How could you possibly pass as a slave.'

'I have the proof burned into my legs,' Clodia said bitterly.

Crassus' eyes dropped to her uncovered ankles on the divan wondering exactly where the brand was. Near her coveted treasure, he'd been told.

'But that would mean considerable embarrassment to you,' he remonstrated. 'And it's possible someone would recognise you in any case.'

'Not if I went dressed as a slave, had my hair cut, made myself unkempt. What slave ever looks up from the ground in Rome, anyway? Nobody would recognise me. I'm sure. As for the others, I no longer care. They could see the scars for their proof.'

Crassus licked his lips. He felt a flutter at his loins.

'They would kill you if you were discovered,' he

said. 'That would be a ridiculous, shameful fate for such a beautiful woman.'

'My fate doesn't worry me,' Clodia said. 'Only that of Spartacus. If they killed me I hope it would not be before I had the pleasure of seeing a dagger in his heart.'

'You are a very brave woman,' Crassus said. He felt a slight frustration. If her fate mattered so little to her, how could a night in his bed be refused him. But her cold beauty repelled any consideration of making advances to her and he contented himself with adding: 'But think such a plan would be madness.'

'Well I offered my services,' Clodia said coldly. 'I am going anyway.'

Crassus stood up from his couch and paced slowly to the window and back.

'If that is so,' he murmured at last, 'then naturally, in spite of my horror at the danger into which you put yourself, I should be foolish to refuse your help.'

'Good,' Clodia said, with finality. 'Then if you'll give me a day to prepare, perhaps you'll then give me an escort to within a reasonable distance of the gladiator's camp and arrange for the safety of my passage when I return.'

'Certainly,' Crassus said. 'I'll give instruction to specially trusted guards on the city walls. You'll have no difficulty.'

Clodia rose. Her eyes had not left his throughout the interview.

'Finally,' she said, 'I would like you not to mention my plans to anyone at all apart from your special guards. I am leaving word with my slaves that I am going north. I'm sure everyone will understand why I should wish to leave the city.'

'You may trust me implicitly,' Crassus assured her. He had in fact the reputation of a man who could keep his mouth shut.

Walking with her towards the door of his house, Crassus cast sidelong glances at the soft swaying of her breasts. But in spite of what he considered her suicidal mission, he could not bring himself to suggest a last night of joy before she went. Perhaps he was afraid of refusal.

'Incidentally,' he said as they walked. 'It is my belief that this man Spartacus is becoming some sort of god among his rabble. With him out of the way I believe half the battle would be won.'

'We shall see.'

He watched the stola, pulled in at her slim waist, writhing gently around her bottom as she walked away.

CHAPTER NINE

When Clodia rode out from the city with the two Roman centurions galloping on either side, her appearance had changed considerably. Her hair had been cropped much shorter and allowed to become unkempt; she wore none of the perfume and adornments of her class. Her lips were unrouged, she wore no powdered antimony around her eyes, no cream on her skin; she was dressed in the dirty tunic of a slave and her nails, even, had been cut and allowed to become impregnated with dirt.

In some strange way these preparations, while altering her appearance, seemed only to add to her beauty, giving her a wild, forest beauty in place of the refined, hothouse loveliness of before.

They rode hard in the darkness, towards the south, their horses' hooves clattering on the stones of the road until it became too risky for the escort to go farther.

At a point in the wilds, Clodia dismounted and watched silently while the men wheeled and disappeared back towards the safety of Rome, taking her horse with them.

Clodia shivered, unaccustomed to the short tunic. And then she began to walk. For some time she kept up a good pace, her sandled feet thudding steadily on the stones.

After an hour or two she was beginning to tire. She had been used to travelling by carriage or in a slave-borne litter. All around her was dark loneliness and she began to feel afraid. It occurred to her that she might not even get to Spartacus' camp, but might be struck down by robbers. She quickened her pace again.

Another hour passed and Clodia felt sure she must be in enemy territory. Antium had been the last town they'd wrecked. They must now have moved farther north.

Her legs ached now and her shoulders responded to the ache with another. She sat down for a while on a roadside tomb, listening to the wind, the night noises of insects, hearing nothing besides. She nearly fell asleep, resisted and began to trudge south once more.

When she suddenly found herself surrounded by a small group of armed men she was startled that she had not heard the slightest sound before they were there.

'It's a woman,' a voice shouted.

There were murmurs of curiosity.

'I am Marcia, slave of Lucius Crispus,' she cried quickly. 'I have come to join Spartacus.'

The men moved in closer. Clodia was not afraid. Many slave women had fled, sometimes with male slaves, sometimes alone, to escape from the cruelty of their patrician masters.

Now she could see the men. They were armed with short swords and some had shields. They were clearly some advance guard of Spartacus' forces.

'Why should you want to join us?' The words had come from a big, bluff man, shaggy as a monkey, with a big moustache. He appeared to be the commander of the group.

'Because I hate the Roman overlords,' Clodia said with a snarl in her voice. 'I want freedom.'

'And what did your overlord do to you, my pretty one?'

'He tried to rape me,' Clodia said boldly.

There were hoots of laughter.

'Only tried!' someone yelled. 'He must have been senile.'

'Shut up! Do you want the Romans to hear us?' snapped the leader.

He came closer to Clodia, examining her in the gloom, from head to toe. His eyes were wary. They had not accepted her without question.

He put his hand on her breast and Clodia felt it there, warm and heavy for a few seconds.

'A beauty, all right,' he said softly. He whistled quietly through his teeth.

'Will you take me back to your camp?' Clodia asked. 'Ive been walking from Rome and I'm exhausted.'

'Let's exhaust her a little more, first,' somebody said.

'Yes. I lay first claim,' said another.

113

The big man turned savagely on them again.

'I said shut up,' he snapped violently.

'What odds? There aren't any Roman soldiers left,' one of his men said petulantly. A titter of laughter greeted his remark.

The big man left Clodia and pushed his way to the speaker. He hit him squarely on the jaw and the man fell backwards and lay holding his face.

Nobody else moved and the big man surveyed them.

'I'm in charge,' he said. 'If I say shut up, everybody shuts up.'

'All right, all right,' they growled around him.

He turned back to Clodia, who, now that she had actually stopped walking again, began to feel weak. She had a sense of anti-climax about the whole thing, a numbness in her head where there should have been fear, determination, some acute reaction to the situation.

The leader's eyes were on her again. She could still feel where he had held her breast as if weighing it.

'Turn around.'

She almost hesitated – and then turned obediently, presenting him with her back.

'Lovely piece of flesh,' someone said. There was a note of awe in the voice.

The big man suddenly gripped her tunic at the shoulder, ripping it across the back. Clodia stood still, trembling slightly. 'Why haven't you any lash marks on your back?' the man snapped.

'He never lashed me,' Clodia said. 'He preferred to slap my face and try to rape me.'

The man grunted and then she felt his hand move down her back and feel her bottom. He cupped his big hand around the buttocks and drew it across her whole rump. She heard the almost inaudible whistle through his teeth again.

'Where are your brand marks?' he asked roughly.

'On my legs.'

'Where? Show them.'

Clodia turned towards the watching men again and pulled up her tunic. Everybody pressed closer; the air resounding with suckings of lips, cluckings of tongues. The big man looked round and pushed them back. 'Give her some room,' he said unnecessarily.

Clodia edged up the hem of her loincloth, stopping short at the verge of her crotch. The little crescents made dark marks on the white skin.

The man nodded. He touched the marks with his finger tips. His fingers were moist on her skin. And then her ran his hand suddenly between her legs, brushing it along the thin curtain of cloth over her vagina.

Clodia breathed in sharply. The feeling of his rough fingers on the thinly-veiled flesh brought home to her what she had let herself in for, seemed to bring back sensation to her mind and body.

The big man chuckled, noticing her reaction.

'All right,' he said. 'Let's go.'

'How about it chief. Let's stretch her out and give her a welcome.'

Clodia was horrified now that she was confronted with the reality, even though she would have to submit to somebody. It was a thought she had hidden

115

in the back of her mind, overwhelming it with her desire for revenge on Spartacus.

The leader seized her arm and turned to the others.

'Listen,' he said. 'This one is mine. I've been looking for something like this for a long time – and if anybody wants to quarrel with that then say so now.'

There was a hostile silence.

'Maybe Spartacus would like to see her – or Marcellus,' someone said threateningly. Clodia's heart fell.

The big man's lip curled savagely under his moustache.

'If anyone thinks that, he can come and take her.'

He released Clodia's arm and stood in a posture of mock invitation. Again nobody moved.

'And if anyone tries to be funny later on,' he added, 'they tell me it's a pretty uninteresting existence in one of those things.' He indicated the dim shape of one of the roadside tombs.

There was no more argument and Clodia was marched with them across the plain to the inland hills. The big man held her arm all the way. Her mind simply refused to react to the thought that she was his.

They were challenged by a number of lookouts on the way and finally passed by the sentries into the gladiator's camp.

The camp was set in a small valley in the foothills of the mountains, well-guarded to the west by the hills with their lookout posts, well-guarded on the other three sides by the height and steepness of the mountains. It was a big camp. It now housed close to ten thousand people. The tents were arranged in neat rows with here and there a clearing where a fire glowed and people sat talking and drinking in the flickering light.

A fresh patrol went out to replace the one which had just come in and the group of men dispersed.

The big man led Clodia through the ranks of tents, stopping finally in front of one. He bent and untied the flaps and stooped into the interior, dragging her with him. He released her while he fussed with something in the darkness. Then the light of a stolen lamp flared up and he fastened the tent flaps behind them.

Removing his helmet and his armour, then unstrapping his sandals, he looked at Clodia. He nodded towards the rough bed and she sat down on it. He continued to look at her as he drew off first one sandal then the the other His eyes lingered on the exposed portions of her legs and thighs. She was the most beautiful slave he'd ever seen.

'You eaten?' he asked.

Clodia shook her head and he indicated a leather pannier.

'Bread and cheese and wine in there,' he said. She was to learn as she came to know him better how sudden flashes of kindness and humour would break through his usual domineering and sadistic attitude.

He never took his eyes from her while she ate. At last he stood up, his great, hairy body bulging mountainously from his loincloth, and took a draught of wine.

'Get undressed,' he snapped.

117

Clodia sat there dumbly while he took off his loin-cloth. His big penis was in full erection, soaring out from his loins like a stiff, artificial fixture. Clodia felt sick. She had known this would have to happen, but somehow she hadn't faced the reality.

He turned towards her and his shaggy testicles swung under the organ which seemed to point accusingly at her.

'I said get your clothes off,' he snapped viciously.

Mechanically, Clodia began to pull off the tunic.

The man sat and watched her, scratching his testicles.

As each article of clothing came off, he whistled through his teeth. Her breasts were so taut and big, the skin looked soft and flawless, different from so many of the women he'd had.

When she slipped out of the loincloth, her heart was thumping and her face was burning with shame. Revenge, revenge, she kept telling herself. This was the only way.

The man smacked his lips.

'Turn around,' he said.

She turned around. He had her turn around several times, looking at her body in admiration and a desire which he increased by not seizing her immediately. He could hardly believe the perfection of the lines of buttocks and breasts, the skin pulled in tautly below the breasts so that the lines of the ribs were light shadows. Her hip! The breath wheezed through his teeth at her hips with their fleshy flowering into thighs and the tufts of central hair that gleamed in the flickering light . . .

118

'Jupiter, what a wonderful piece you're going to be,' he muttered.

Clodia turned away, overcome by the coarseness of his tone. Her stomach was heaving in and out, her breasts rising and falling in a constricted pain.

'This lord of yours must have been a woman,' he cracked.

He got heavily to his feet and came over to her. He pressed hard up against her and she could feel his great club hot against her buttocks. His big hands closed over her breasts as he pressed her back against him. He kissed her neck, his hot breath panting over into her face, his moustache tickling her.

In his arms, Clodia felt crushed. She had a peculiar revulsion in her loins which was half excitement. He was like an animal, a great hairy beast. She felt his hand wander down from her breasts, feeling her body, pressing on the stomach, the abdomen. And as he pressed on her lower belly, she felt his hips pushing into her, felt herself pulled back onto his penis.

'Lie down on the bed,' he ordered thickly.

Clodia lay on the bed, her eyes closed.

'On your belly,' he snarled impatiently.

Clodia's lips moved in a prayer as she rolled over onto her belly. She clutched the blankets with her hand, pushing her face into the rough sacking he used as a pillow.

She heard the breath whistle through his teeth again as he stood looking down at her for a moment. She heard a shuffle, sensed him bending towards her and then his great hairy body seemed to envelop her,

119

crushing her into the rough blankets. He did not blow out the lamp.

Clodia tried to forget herself. She tried to imagine that perhaps it was Spartacus and that she no longer hated him. But the filthy wheezings would not allow her to forget that this was an animal, a great, uncouth, shaggy animal using her delicate body. She was afraid, too, of the pain of being used in this disgusting way. She wished she could faint.

She cringed under his shuffling hips. She could feel the thick, curly hair of his loins, brushing warmly on her bottom. She clasped her buttocks together, hopelessly.

His fingers tugged her hair so that she gave a little shriek, muffled in the blankets.

'Open your legs,' he commanded.

He tugged her hair again, viciously, panting with a mixture of annoyance and passion. She squealed and spread her thighs automatically.

The man slithered between them. She forced herself to relax. It was no good fighting him.

She felt his fingers pressing, at last, against her tender flesh and she jerked her hips involuntarily into the blankets.

'Relax,' he snarled.

She relaxed again and his fingers were prodding the tight, tender skin. She felt the blunt, hot hugeness of him there now as his hips jerked and shuffled on her.

He was muttering fiercely, wheezing through his teeth. He did not penetrate. His breath was a series of gasps. Suddenly he slithered up from her, kneeling between her thighs.

He pulled her hips off the blankets, up towards him.

'Kneel up, kneel up!' he cursed.

Reluctant and frightened, she kneeled up. She felt his knees pushing her knees further from each other. A tremour went through her body at being treated this way. It seemed unreal.

She felt his hands on her waist, pressing down, forcing her back to arch concavely. She flopped her hot face down on the sacking. Her bottom seemed to be something apart from her, right up in the air, exposed behind her.

Looking down on her, the big man was twisted with passion at the beauty of her body. He was aching to get in her with a passion that shook his whole body.

As he pushed forward, he began to pull her bottom back as well, grasping her hips at the soft, creased flesh where her thighs joined them, feeling her soft belly trembling beneath his finger tips.

He undulated his hips, pushing, pushing, stabbing, and suddenly there was a give.

Crying noiselessly into the sacking, Clodia felt his thickness suddenly invade her with the sharp pain of a sword thrust. She couldn't bear it. She tried to struggle away, but he held her hips in a fury of passion and kept his knees between her thighs. Her breasts brushed against the blankets so that her aching nipples hurt against the rough texture.

She cried out, biting into the sacking, her hands twisting the blankets into ridges. She felt as if she wanted to be sick. Gradually she became used to the filling. It was just a terrible, degrading soreness which flared into a new pain each time he thrust forward. Clodia cried abandonedly into the sacking. This was the final indignity.

The fact of her crying and clutching the blankets added to his passion. It was like a blind spot in his head. His head was passion. There was nothing else in it.

He grasped her hips so hard that his fingers dug deeply into the flesh. He pulled her hips back at him every time he jerked forward, so that she helplessly assisted in the further impalement. He had never known such exquisite pain.

He stabbed hard at her and she tried to jerk forward again. He could see her flaming cheeks, the tears spilling on the sacking, feel the stomach heaving like a mad thing. And then he rammed forward with all his might.

That was it. His lips pulled away from his teeth as he looked at her helpless body, writhing under him. A fury was in his loins. He pulled almost right out of her and then pushed stiffly in again the whole way.

Clodia was unable to think. Her body was no longer hers. It belonged to him and he was using it, abusing it, she wished she had not set out on this mad mission. She cried out inside herself, mouth working against the sacking, feeling the salt of her tears on her lips. She could no longer escape. She was held too firmly. She had to remain grotesquely positioned, to be skewered and skewered until he reached his finish and it was over.

His panting was faster, becoming uncontrolled. It filled the tent, resonating from the walls. His hips jerked with rapid fury. His heart was thumping so loudly in his chest that he could hear it. His loins were an inferno of sensation. The sensation seemed to swim round and round in them aimlessly while he gasped and screwed up his face in passion.

Round and round, jostling, flowing in his loins. And then he felt it gain direction. He pressed her waist down towards the blankets, and he heard her muffled gasping.

The hot, burning liquid was flowing now, coming to the outer world like an erupting volcano. He slowed to grinding thrusts, trying to savour the last delights. And then his mouth opened wide and he could no longer control, only yield, and the volcano had erupted.

He lay on her, crushing her, breathing heavily and she kept still under his weight. Her body felt exhausted, emotionally she felt exhausted. She wanted badly to sleep and forget.

After a while he rolled off her and lay, face up, on the bed. Soon she heard him snoring and she breathed a sigh of relief; then she, too, relaxed, and in spite of everything, her mind sank into comforting oblivion.

She was awakened much later, by his big hands which were wandering over her body, up her back. She was forced to turn over and open her thighs to receive him again. She was having to pay dearly for her revenge.

CHAPTER TEN

Marcus Crassus sat thoughtfully on the lowest marble tier of the circus. It was the first time he had been to see the chariot races for some time. In fact lately he'd found himself doing a number of things he'd not been used to doing.

The legions were nearly ready now. He'd made good pay offers and managed so far to organise some five legions – close on 35,000 men.

Apart from this work of organisation he'd been able to concentrate only on unimportant and rather frivolous happenings. The races fell under this category as far as he was concerned.

Crassus was well aware to what his restlessness was due. Always his thoughts returned to the same thing, the same image – Clodia. Many times he had cursed his cowardice in not making an open suggestion to her that they have a night of love. After all, with such a dangerous future she might have decided to give herself over to a last night of pleasure. It was highly probable that on arriving at the rebel camp she would have to submit to some coarse fellow and at least

Crassus had breeding. He felt ridiculously jealous that some stupid slave should possess Clodia while the exquisite delight should be denied him. And then, at worst, she would simply have refused. Her life in Rome, as she herself had said, was finished. She could have made no difficulty for him.

At night he pictured her body, stripped her slowly of her clothes, imagined their first advances and then practically had an orgasm at the thought of her writhing and moaning beneath him. Again he pictured Spartacus having her – he was now convinced of the affair. How had she been? Enthusiastic, obviously. He tried to imagine her throwing the whole fervour of her beauty into their lovemaking. Then, in turn, he pictured Marcellus, having her on a couch in front of patrician Rome, with Clodia lying nude and motionless. He felt an itch at his loins, and sighed.

He looked round the circus, up at the crowds balanced on their wooden tiers behind him, all shouting, betting, gossiping, flirting. He decided he would make a bet, otherwise he was afraid he'd see the stallions fade into a picture of Clodia as he watched.

The races today were the trial of some fresh horses from Spain. Crassus forced Clodia from his mind and allowed himself to be carried on the great surge of excitement which filled the circus.

Below him the track was neat, the sand freshly replenished and raked. On the embankment in the centre, which joined the two posts around which the chariots would whirl, were the seven large wooden eggs. The attendant who would remove one as each

125

lap was completed, was fussily arranging and rearranging them.

In the open boxes at the western end of the track, the twelve chariots glinted in the sun, and the horses jostled gently and whinnied. A soft breeze wafted through the circus.

Crassus had begun to drift off again into the rebel tents and the pictures of Clodia being ravished – perhaps, even, in more places than one – when he was brought back to the present by the white napkin, fluttering down into the arena from the hand of the Consul.

A trumpet sounded the start and the Consul sat down, draping his embroidered Tyrian toga over his scarlet tunic, while a slave steadied the heavy wreath of golden leaves on his head.

As the ropes, stretched between the marble Hermes on each side of the boxes, fell away, a wild excitement seized the scores of thousands of people in the circus. They could enjoy themselves now. The legions were almost ready to depart. They were estimated to outnumber the gladiators' forces by at least three to one.

The dust flew beneath the chariot wheels as the competitors raced for the first bend.

Crassus studied the horses. They were certainly fine animals. Their breast-plates studded with plaques and amulets, their manes starred with pearls, gave them a glorious appearance.

He searched for the red ribbons around the horses' necks. That was the colour of the party he'd backed.

Crassus had always marvelled at these charioteers.

These men, who, like the gladiators, often started from slaves. With success they became practically the playboys of Rome – although they were never invited to the houses of the noblemen. They were the heroes of the masses of the city.

Crassus had gained such power as he had by his scheming brain, his power of manipulation. He was not essentially a man of action, a public hero, a man whose physique and cool strength of mind made him an imposing figure. He wished he could have inherited the courage of a charioteer to go with his other useful qualities. Nothing could have stopped him then in his ambition to control men's lives.

His eyes flicked over the charioteers. He could make them out through the dust and swirling of horses. Their helmets shone, whips flashed, their coloured tunics were cut in half by the binding reins which would be slashed by a dagger to release them from the horses if there was a crash.

The crowd was already shouting with excitement by the time one egg had been removed from the central embankment. A charioteer of the green faction was going neck and neck with the red. Their horses raced, snorting, nostrils flared side by side, the chariots swung towards each other and then away again. Behind them thundered the rest of the field in a fluid pattern.

Both chariots turned well. The two outside horses, attached not to the shaft but by traces, had been well trained. The inside one acted as a vital pivot as the offside horse swung out.

Crassus felt his blood stirring. Women were

127

screaming with excitement on the terraces. If he had the nerve of a charioteer he could have had Clodia before she left. He wouldn't have worried about being rebuffed. He wouldn't have laughed and made some coarse witticism without turning a hair. How he envied them that cool quality!

Another egg had gone down, and another.

The fluid pattern shifted. The green chariot swung out too far on a corner and a white one shot inside next to the red. They raced, three abreast, along the straight side below where the Consul watched; the wheels scraped as they wheeled around the far bend and then the white was firmly established beside the red and the green had fallen back.

Crassus began to take a partisan interest in the red. After all he had backed it. If it won, he told himself, he would have Clodia yet. Yet, this was the omen.

Four, five eggs down and still the red was there on the inside – a winning position if it could be maintained until the final bend.

And then disaster. Hugging the turning post too close at a bend, the red chariot crashed into it. The wheel caught and tipped in crashing. The crowds shrieked. There was the flash of the charioteer's dagger and the chariot had turned over, dragging half the horses with it.

The charioteer who had crashed off the back, lay where he was, arms over his head as the following chariots swerved to avoid the tangle.

As the last of the remainder swept around the bend, attendants rushed to right the frightened, but unharmed horses and drag them away to the boxes before the return of the throng.

The charioteer was helped to his feet and carried to the embankment. He was lucky to have escaped with only a broken leg.

Of course, there was always that, Crassus thought, in the disappointment of the wrecking of his omen. They came to grief. They were brave, their nerves and bodies were of iron, but these qualities which led them into such exciting and dangerous callings were so frequently their undoing. The death rate among charioteers was considerable. Often the most successful was killed in his prime, when his glory could not have been greater.

The chariots thundered on in a close mass, the white in the sole lead now.

Another egg down – a last circuit with its two bends to go.

And now, from the mass of flying hooves and wheels, surging out from the dust and the roar, the second red driver emerged.

Crassus had given him no chance. The man had been left at the start. But now he had moved up, lost in the middle of the throng, suddenly to leap forward.

The white chariot hugged the embankment as the red drew away by a fraction of a wheel from the remainder. The whip flew in the charioteer's hand, the horses panted and thundered.

At the last bend but one the red-ribboned horses had drawn level with the chariot ahead and the crowds were shouting themselves hoarse.

The leading charioteer glanced sideways at the

oncoming horses. He had thought himself well away. That glance took his eyes for a moment from his stallions and the track ahead. His wheel caught the embankment and the chariot rocked and skidded. The frightened horses, feeling the pull, slowed. The driver lashed them forward again as the chariot righted itself from the near disaster – but it was too late. His red opponent had shot smoothly ahead and taken the bend well, cutting in to the inside position.

The crowd rose to its feet as the red chariot raced along the inside and took the last bend with ease. The white chariot was a length behind. The result was a foregone conclusion.

As the leading chariot flashed past the winning line, cheers rocked the hills on which the terraces rose.

Crassus was astonished and pleased. He would have Clodia. And then he laughed at himself for such fantasies. But he was still pleased that the red had won.

Chattering broke out along the terraces, expert discussion of the qualities of the new horses and of the rider who had won so unexpectedly. Winnings were gathered and bets placed for the next race.

During the interval a programme of acrobatic tricks was shown. This was almost as great an attraction as the races themselves. Jockeys guided two horses at once, leaping from one to the other with perfect control. Others snatched pieces of cloth from the track at full gallop; others, even more versed, seized swords without suffering a scratch. Yet others made mimic war on horseback with blunted weapons until one was toppled to the soft, sand-covered ground.

And finally the arena was cleared and the next race was ready to begin.

A dozen races were scheduled in all to cover the day. Some were simply horseback races, others chariot races with two, three or even ten horses taking the place of the more usual four.

Crassus thought of Clodia through the intervals, stretching his red-sandaled feet in the sun, adjusting his purple-striped toga. During the races he imagined that if his colour won he would have her in this circumstance or that.

It was towards the end of the day when one of his trusted freedmen came to him and whispered that the lady, Clodia Crispus, had arrived at his house and was waiting to see him.

As if aroused from a dream to find that it was actually true, Crassus rose, adjusted his toga once again, and strode after his attendant, leaving the roar of the crowd behind him as yet another race came to a whirlwind close.

CHAPTER ELEVEN

It had taken Clodia only a few days to learn that her owner in the gladiator's camp was one of Spartacus' minor lieutenants – which meant that he was kept well-abreast of future plans.

He had used her body in every imaginable way in that short time and then, under her encouragement, finding her interested and intelligent, he had begun to confide in her.

The gladiators had heard of Crassus' plans to organise an army to fight them and they intended to watch for its departure from Rome, attempt to skirt its southward march through the hills, leaving, perhaps, a minor contingent to maintain the illusion of the camp, and then take Rome.

The legions would return as soon as they realised the trick that had been played on them, her master, Martius, informed her, and then they could be beaten slowly and systematically while they attempted to besiege the newly-fallen city.

'A very clever idea,' Clodia commented. 'This is your leader, Spartacus' strategy?'

Martius' eyes took on a glint of respect and deference as he nodded.

'He is a great man,' he said. 'Without him we'd be a number of aimless, wandering parties – easy meat for the soldiers. Who'd ever have thought we could have taken Rome?'

'Who indeed?' said Clodia.

It had become clear to her, too, over the last few days, that Spartacus – whom she'd not seen – was treated more as a god than a human being among his men. He was the brains behind every move. His were the cool eyes which filled every member of his band who looked at him with an overwhelming confidence. As long as Spartacus was there, not only was there hope, but almost undoubted success, was the feeling.

Clodia remembered his big, muscular body and that strong face. It seemed a long time since she'd seen him, but his image was still vivid in her memory. Her desire for revenge was still deep.

During the day, she worked with the other women, grinding corn, washing clothes in a stream, chatting, hiding successfully her birthright, learning about the future movements and the awe in which their leader was held.

During the night she submitted to the careless and violent intercourse of Martius – all in the cause of learning still more on her path of revenge.

On the day that Marcus Crassus was watching his red charioteer race to victory, Clodia learned that Martius was to go on night patrol.

That evening, taking her life in her hands, she crept from the camp with Martius' horse, rode like the wind across the plains below the foothills, eventually joining the road at what she considered a safe distance, and thundered up the Appian Way to Rome.

The sun was sinking towards dusk as she was received by one of Crassus' special guards who were kept permanently on duty to await her arrival.

She was escorted quietly through the back streets where small shops were still selling their wares and bawdy houses were rocking with laughter and song, to Marcus Crassus' house where she was made comfortable to await his arrival.

Hurrying towards his mansion in the wake of his attendant, Crassus felt a nervous excitement bubbling inside him. He was much less concerned about what news Clodia might bring than the possibility of possessing her – a fact which astonished him. He wondered if he had the choice whether he would be prepared to risk Rome before the gladiator horde if, in return, it meant that he might have the woman he so desired. He found no ready answer.

He found Clodia still in the unkempt, but wildly beautiful role of the slave. She looked tired and her eyes had taken on an unemotional, fatalistic expression. He wondered exactly what she'd been through the last few days.

She rose to greet him and he kissed her hand.

'My dear lady, I'm very happy to see you. I had fears that dreadful things might have befallen you.'

'They have – but no matter,' Clodia said without expression.

She was wrapped in a toga which had been found for her in the house. Crassus felt a twinge of excite-

134

ment run through him at her words. He fought down a desire to beg her to tell him what had happened to her.

'You have news?' he asked. But before she could answer he recolled his duties as host.

'I beg your pardon – my excitement at learning the latest situation at the gladiators' camp got the better of me. Have you eaten? I will have a meal brought to you straight away.'

Clodia dismissed his hospitality with a wave of her hand.

'Thanks. I have eaten,' she said. 'After I have given you what information I have, perhaps I might be allowed to bathe.'

'Most certainly,' Crassus said. 'Anything at all you wish.'

'When will the legions be ready?' Clodia asked.

'In two or three days. We are still trying to recruit . . .'

'Good. Well, at the time they pass through the gates of Rome, a band of Spartacus' scouts will be watching.'

'That is to be expected,' Crassus said. 'I trust their report will make him feel a new respect for Rome.'

Clodia cut him short, impatiently.

'Not at all,' she said. 'It will simply give him the signal to move quickly north through the foothills, leaving a small company in his camp.

'By this manouevre he hopes to outflank Rome and move in to the attack while the legions are hunting for the scattering remnants of the camp far to the south. He thinks he will be able to take Rome without too much difficulty and be well established by the time the legions return.'

Crassus whistled.

'The man's audacity is astonishing,' he said slowly. 'How big are his forces?'

'He has close on ten thousand well armed men.'

Crassus whistled again.

'We have been very badly served with information hitherto,' he said. 'I would have put the figure at half that and thought them badly armed into the bargain.'

'Their army is a formidable one,' Clodia said. 'Every day, the gladiators take cohorts of slaves and teach them how to fight. They give them instruction in how to deal with the special tactics and formation of the legions, too.'

'And every man with everything to gain, nothing to lose,' Crassus mused. 'This is not a very pretty picture. This man Spartacus must have some spark of genius in him.'

'How will you meet them, now?' Clodia asked.

Crassus thought for a moment.

'Naturally the details will need some attention,' he said. 'But in broad principle we'll send out only two of the legions we've organised. We're hoping to have seven by the time we're ready so that'll leave some 30,000 troops in the city – more than enough to surprise Spartacus and his crew. As for the other two, we'll dispatch a fast messenger as soon as the gladiators appear. They should be back in time for any possible hitches or – let us confidently hope – the last skirmishes.'

'It won't be any simple matter even then,' Clodia

said. 'So to achieve my aim, and perhaps spare a few Roman lives, I, too, have a plan which may be of some assistance.'

'Pray go on,' Crassus invited.

'I intend to kill Spartacus before his massed troops as he advanced on the city,' Clodia said.

Crassus was dumbstruck. The thought of the Thracian leader simply being struck down by a woman in the midst of his force – after all the power and destruction he had wielded and wrought – was beyond his comprehension.

'But – but . . .'. And then he smiled. 'This is madness my dear. You have done wonderful work. You have almost undoubtedly saved Rome from this barbarian. All Rome shall honour you. But as for this plan, it really can't be considered. It's impossible. And even were it possible, it would be suicide.'

He took her hand comfortingly, and a distracting cloud passed behind his eyes at the soft touch of her hand in his, her beautiful face so close.

'You have had a hard time,' he said. 'You must rest. Spartacus will meet his doom anyway. I offer you the hospitality of my house in all discretion if you wish to rest for some days.'

Clodia did not bother to withdraw her hand. She let it rest in the pudgy fingers of the banker. His catching her hand had turned her attention to him for the moment. It was as if she saw for the first time the man who was going to defeat the army which Spartacus had built.

She looked into the gleaming eyes under their heavy lids, set in the gross, overfed face with its clean-shaven skull. This fat, wretched man was going to head five legions to the destruction of Spartacus' army. The thought made her slightly sick. She thought of Spartacus, strong and handsome and magnetic, his courage giving out confidence to his men and again she wished it could have been different.

'There is no difficulty,' she said, with quiet resignation. 'I shall muffle myself in the clothes of one of his minor lieutenants. That should enable me to get close to him. I shall strike him down with his lieutenant's sword, or perhaps with a dagger. After that I don't care. They will have no time to do more than kill me and I may even manage to escape to the Roman lines.'

Crassus saw that she intended to carry out her plan. He hated the thought of such a beautiful woman walking into such certain death.

'You are too lovely a woman to do this,' he said passionately. 'All Rome would abhor your decision.'

'All Rome makes me sick,' Clodia retorted. 'Can't you see the additional advantage you would have from this. Spartacus is divine in the eyes of his men. He has become like the Pharaohs, only his divinity is augmented by the natural veneration they feel for him, the confidence his power gives them. Without him they will be thrown into confusion. They will fight. Oh, yes, they will fight. But they will lose the belief in their victory which they have when he is fighting at their head. They will be routed in half the time and with half the danger to the Roman troops.'

Crassus had listened to her with further astonishment. Her insight was considerable. It was true that he also had heard that Spartacus was blessed with the protective hand of a god. It was easily believable that all she said was true. It would provide the final, shattering blow after the presence of the Roman legions.

'I think such a plan has small hope of success,' he said. 'Surely you will be noticed before you have time to strike. Surely they will see you are a woman.'

'It will succeed. Don't worry,' Clodia said.

'And how will you get the clothes and the horse of one of his lieutenants?'

'I shall kill him first,' Clodia replied.

Crassus stared at her in growing astonishment. Truly this woman wanted her revenge more than anything else, more than anyone he'd ever known. He thought of the intrigues he'd know, political, military, commercial, politico-military, the jealousies, tricks, knaveries, vengeances. He could think of nothing to equal this for sheer, daring ruthlessness and fatalistic acceptance of one's own destruction.

He had let her hand drop in his surprise, but now he seized it again in both of his.

'I can't let you do this. It is a ridiculous sacrifice,' he remonstrated.

'Why should you care?' she asked.

'Because it is a sin to deprive men of your beauty.'

'Men have enjoyed my beauty enough in the last few weeks.'

Still holding her hand in his, Crassus pressed it to his lips. With his heart thumping he took the plunge.

'Would you not share that beauty with me for a while before you go, if your mind is really made up?'

139

Clodia looked at the gross man, clutching her hand, the man who was going to try to cut a brave figure in front of Spartacus. She felt a twinge of pity for him in her loathing. She withdrew her hand.

'I no longer have the energy to be insulted,' she said. 'The answer is no.'

To Marcus Crassus this seemed a ridiculous injustice, an unnecessary refusal to give him what would be such bliss. What difference could it make to her if she were determined to die in a few days anyway? He felt somehow robbed of his masculinity, another failure in the light of the courageous, conquering figure he would like to be.

'Very well,' he said.

'I would like to bathe, now,' Clodia said. 'I haven't a lot of time.'

'I'll show you the way,' Crassus said.

He led her through the quadrilateral and into the bath building. As they reached it she slipped off her toga. He opened the door for her to pass through. Her breasts seemed to move under his very eyes, hillocks of tight tunic, pushing out from her body. He caught his breath.

'You'll find all you need in there,' he said.

'Thank you,' she replied.

He watched her for a second, with her buttocks pressing against the tunic, as she walked, in an impudent rippling. His eyes travelled quickly down her long, slim legs and back to the sinuous movement of the bottom. He closed the door quietly behind her and stood there trembling.

Inside the baths, Clodia removed her tunic, her brassiere, her loincloth, and walked down the steps into the warm water of the pool. The water moved up her body like a lover's hand, embracing her thighs, hips and at last her breasts. It was soothing, relaxing. She stood letting the steam soak into her pores. It seemed that all the horrors of the last few weeks – or was it months or years – were being gently, luxuriously washed away.

It was in the baths, she recalled, that the whole business had actually begun to take shape. But for her original desire, there may have been no escape of the gladiators, no raping of patricians, killing of their menfolk, no razing of cities.

She sighed. It was impossible to think that all of that had been her doing.

Clodia floated off on the water. This was luxury. Except for the ache in her loins, it washed away everything – all the dirt, lust, beastliness, shame of the last few days. The baths were a wonderful institution – as good as sleep.

She noticed the couches around the bath, the gold encrusted in the marble mosaic. Crassus was reputed to be the richest man in the Empire. He had virtually proven it with his equipping of the new legions.

What a nerve the man had! But then her anger dissipated, listlessly. How could she feel angry at his suggestion after what she'd been through. That was what every man wanted when he looked at her. Though she couldn't remember if Spartacus had so much as looked at her before she'd made advances to him.

Spartacus. She tried to remember his touch, the way he had been that night in her room. That was the last sex she had enjoyed, had needed. She felt a slight gnawing in her stomach. She had to kill him. That was the only way. The only hope for her.

She climbed out of the bath and began to dry herself on a cloth. She dried her face, neck, shoulders, dabbed her breasts and belly, towelled her back and rubbed her buttocks. She put one foot on a couch to run the cloth down her thigh. A noise disturbed her. She looked up to see Crassus just inside the door, naked and in a state of obvious sexual excitement.

Crassus had started to leave the baths, but the desire to have Clodia was too excruciating. Across the quadrilateral he had stopped. Little drops of perspiration gathered on his forehead and on his upper lip. It was dark now. It was now or never, he told himself. A fresh image of Clodia formed in his mind, an image of her retreating from the bath, with the tunic outlining those firm buttocks.

Who would know? He could spread the word she had joined the rebels.

He looked at the building. Lights were on in the kitchen quarters. That was all.

He walked slowly back to the baths. His heart was thumping, his stomach trembling. Once he made the move he'd have to go through with it. The image of Clodia formed again, almost restricting his breathing.

Gently he pushed open the door of the baths and peered in to where the lamps glowed through the steam. Clodia had her back half towards him. Her leg was raised, foot resting on a couch while she dried herself.

He stared at the delicate sweep of buttocks, the long, well-shaped thighs and calves. The breast he could see was superbly tilted, crowned by a large, jutting nipple which would be hard under the fingers.

Crassus fingered his penis through the toga. He could feel its heat through the cloth. He never wore underclothes.

Crassus slipped inside the door, closing it softly. He couldn't help himself now. He was in sexual torment.

Standing just inside the door he pulled off his toga. As it rustled to the floor, Clodia turned and saw him. Her eyes were astonished and then cold.

'Get out of here,' she said sharply.

Crassus walked towards her, his eyes roving over her naked body. His penis preceded his fat belly by several thick-fleshed inches. The steam mingled with the perspiration of desire on his forehead.

'You must, Clodia,' he pleaded. 'You must.'

Clodia glared at him furiously.

'Don't you dare touch me,' she snapped.

'This is the last time you may ever make love with a man,' Crassus begged. 'Surely you can't be so cruel.'

Clodia felt a great tide of fury and indignation well up inside her.

'You fat, loathsome slug,' she hissed. 'For the last several days I've been raped, raped, you understand? I had to permit it because it was the only way to get what I wanted.

'And I'm tired of it, do you see? I want no more of it. So get out, you disgusting beast.'

Crassus had stopped short at the beginning of her tirade. But the words had simply inflamed him. A violent shiver ran through him and he came on towards her.

'Now that I've seen you, I can't live without having you,' he said.

His pudgy hands reached out for her. Clodia pushed him away, turned to run around the bath and slipped on the marble floor.

In a moment his great fat body was on her, his fat flesh enveloping her.

Crassus felt like crying with delight. She struggled but he hardly noticed. His lips were on hers. He kissed her lips with a hard, moist pressure, smelling the soft bath smell of her skin, feeling her flesh wriggling under his.

'Clodia, Clodia,' he panted. 'You must, you must. Don't struggle.'

'Oh, you beast.' Clodia scratched and bit. The others she had allowed to happen. This was her rape by a fellow-patrician. He thought so little of her esteem, her dignity, that he, Marcus Crassus, whom she had helped, was trying to rape her. Was there no end to man's lust, his brutality?

She struggled out from under him, tried to break away again. But he clambered up after her, grabbing her thighs, rising to his feet, holding her from behind.

All the time he panted: 'Clodia, Clodia. Oh Clodia!' like a maniac.

Weakened from the exhaustion of the preceding days, Clodia felt herself being pushed and half carried to one of the couches.

She tried to kick it away with her feet, but then he had forced her over it and was holding her on it face down.

Crassus was in a delirium. His belly was churned up with desire. He held Clodia down on the couch and half lay on her, half stood behind her. His great penis was on a level with her buttocks, and still breathing, 'Clodia, Clodia,' he forced her struggling legs apart, shuffled between them.

He saw before his blank, desire-filled eyes, the folds of flesh around her vagina, and a giant hand was squeezing his belly, nervous currents shivering all over his body.

He was so excited he could hardly direct his trembling penis. He ranged it, unable to believe that this was true. He was about to have Clodia. This was what he'd dreamed of for days. He breathed her name once again and then buried himself in her vagina.

Crassus moaned with delight and fulfilment on the very first entry. It was an unbelievable relief. All the time of wanting Clodia, picturing Clodia, was coming out now as he thrust into her.

She continued to struggle, but sheer fire, now, helped him to hold her without effort, his hands on her shoulders, his weight on her back.

His great belly rolled on her buttocks as he drove in and in again. His emotion seemed to sing in his head. There was a release of emotion in his loins as he stabbed and ground into her. It had to go on now to the climax, nothing could stop it. And he felt a wild, shattering thankfulness that it was so.

145

'Oh, Clodia. Oh, Clodia. Oh, oh, oh!' he continued to moan. His organ was well within her.

He moved his hands from her shoulders, which trembled now with indignation, and pushed them under her breasts on the couch. He ran them over the beautiful, glossy, budding globes as his thighs pressed her thighs wide and he rammed deeply into her body.

'Clodia,' he begged. 'It's too wonderful. Don't struggle, please. Please!'

Lying under him, stretched over the couch so that her face looked over one edge and her feet reached down almost to the floor on the other, Clodia found her struggles to be of no avail. She heard Crassus' words as he filled her with that heavy, pulsating slug between his legs. She hated him, loathed him. But suddenly her loathing took on a fury at his stupid pleadings. The dolt, she thought. Why didn't he rape her without trying to beg her forgiveness at the same time? Lying passive, feeling his penis worming in long, smooth strokes right up inside her so that it made her wriggle slightly with the sensation, she thought that after all what did it matter now? Who cared? The last time. Might as well let him have what he wanted.

She jerked her bottom furiously back at him as he moved into her channel once more.

Marcus Crassus kissed her neck as his passion grew. Then he leaned up from her, leaving only his hands on her waist, standing on the marble floor, his loins between her thighs. His hips jerked at her in a steady motion. He was transported to a heaven of delight.

She had stopped struggling. Something had happened to her. Now she was wriggling like a hundred snakes under him, pressing her bottom close against his belly, rubbing it against him as he speared into her moist depths.

He gasped with his excitement, tears stood in his eyes. 'Clodia, Clodia,' he uttered.

This was undreamed-of bliss. And she was undulating her hips in cooperation.

He felt the prickling in his loins and slowed. He didn't want to hurry.

He worked up slowly again in a burning delight. He intended to slow and start again for a long time. He would have liked to go on like this forever.

But this time, his passion was too much for him. He went beyond the stage where he could control it.

Clodia was lying there, squirming beneath him and her body was a waiting receptacle to give him relief, to accept the heavy load which was now an embarrassment to him in his desire to be released from it.

Clodia heard him gasping furiously, felt his strokes quicken and then slow, felt him shuffle in towards her so that even the couch moved forward slightly as he tried to get further into her. She pushed her hips back at him, feeling excited, but knowing that she would not reach a climax.

Crassus was on the verge of completion. This was the unbelievable moment. Clodia prostrate, he possessing her. He felt the confined forces trying to break through. He gasped and shouted her name in his passion. There was a moment while the walls held and then the confinement fell away and the sperm of years, it seemed, was flying into Clodia's belly in a flow of never-ending, red-hot shafts.

147

CHAPTER TWELVE

Clodia lay on the tent-bed watching Martius lace his sandals. He was off to the last conference the minor lieutenants would have with Spartacus before the attack. Word had come that the Roman legions were massing outside the gates of Rome in preparation for their march to the south. The camp was a bustle of activity.

'Wait here until I come back,' Martius commanded. 'Then you can ride with me to see the first call of Rome.'

'I'll wait,' Clodia said.

She lay, relaxed, on the rough blankets thinking what a thin line divided the civilised man, the Crassus, from the barbarian, the Martius. Even if she kept her life, she could not, now, go back to Rome. In the desperate last moments of life what had happened between Crassus and herself had seemed unimportant. But she knew that if things returned to normal, she would never forgive herself, or him. She had no clear idea of what to do.

She had not seen Spartacus since she had joined

the camp. It was eerie to think that Martius, who a few hours before had lain on her, possessing her as Spartacus had done, should now be standing before his leader, receiving final instructions.

Outside it was growing dark, the hour that the Romans would be expected to make a rapid march to the south to quell the rebels.

She began to roll the blankets and collect the few things that Martius would need. She was glad she was going with him to within sight of Rome. Otherwise she would have had to kill him now, increasing the chances of her detection.

Outside was the continual clinking of weapons, rustling of tents and clothes, winnying of horses, buzzing of voices. Spartacus had decreed that women were to form the main force to stay behind. Only the lieutenants could take their women with them.

In charge of the women he would leave a few hundred men. Fires were to be built high as an indication of life and a few horsed sentries would shoot a few arrows at the vanguard of the Roman troops before making a get-away. For the rest, as the Roman troops began to cross the wooded plain to the foothills, those in the camp would flee north in the footsteps of the main body. It was thus hoped that by the following evening every man and woman would be safely barricaded behind the walls of Rome.

Clodia looked up as Martius returned He smacked her happily across the rump. He was in a good mood.

'Well, we're off,' he said. 'And woe betide Pompeius when he returns from Spain.'

Pulling down the tent with him, loading it onto the

baggage horses, Clodia felt for a second that she was too small a thing to carry the responsibility for the betrayal of all these people. But the moment passed.

'Where is Spartacus?' she asked.

'Oh, he'll be ready. Don't worry. Do you want to go and kiss him good luck?' Martius guffawed at his own humour.

Spartacus, with Marcellus riding at his side, led the gladiators from the camp and north through the foothills. He had dispatched more scouts to watch the progress of the legions. His first observers had told him the Romans numbered only a couple of legions which had struck him as a rather weak effort. He had expected the sons of Rome to flock to the eagles in greater numbers. Marcellus had been all for waylaying the legions and entering pitched battled with them. But he had crushed that idea. It was pointless losing men in open battle when they could fight from the security of the city's walls.

Behind him, his army streamed, some riding, the majority marching. It was a difficult path through the foothills, a tiring one. But he had promised them all a rest within sight of Rome. Now it was necessary to hurry. They should see Rome by daybreak.

His mouth set in a grim smile as he thought of Rome. What would it be like to live in Rome as its lord? How would it be to own the city? He would do away with the gladiator fights. He would try to encourage something on the style of the Grecian Olympic Games, which he'd heard about. Those who were the backbone of bloodlust in the masses would have to accustom themselves to another form of sport.

150

He would do his best for the people, but the patricians would suffer. Some he would keep on the Senate, to guide him, but he would give no opportunity for corruption or revolt.

He pulled himself back to the present with a jerk. He was not yet inside the walls of Rome.

He wondered about Clodia who had started all this, who was going to bring about the downfall of Rome. He had hardly thought of her for some time. But now, with the entry into Rome at hand, he wondered how she had recovered from her shame, whether she had left Rome. Perhaps as lord of the city – and later of the Empire – he would seek her out and make her his woman. There would be few in the new city who would then regard her with anything but envy.

He looked back through the dusk at the thin lines of low torches. They were making good progress.

'We'll have a banquet in the forum tomorrow night,' he said to Marcellus.

'I'll have roast senator,' Marcellus grinned.

Riding on the back of Martius' horse, along the flank of the scrambling, slipping body of men, Clodia could see ahead the torch borne by somebody in Spartacus' group. She could not see Spartacus, however, as the light the torches threw was dim, only sufficient to light up the few paces ahead of horses and men.

She clutched Martius around his leather Roman overtunic. In the sheath at his side was the sword with which she would kill him. She felt a smouldering pity for him for a few seconds. He was happy at the moment. He was going into the sort of activity he

151

loved, the only sort of activity he really understood and felt for.

At intervals the horde was intercepted by scouts. The word got to the lieutenants that they were now parallel with the legions, separated only by darkness, a few miles of plain and a range of foothills.

Martius chuckled.

'Picture their faces when they find out,' he roared. 'I'd give my horse to see them.

'How is Rome to be taken?' Clodia asked, leaning forward, raising her voice against the clacking of the horses' hooves.

'Very straightforward,' Martius replied over his shoulder. 'At daybreak we'll just move forward in a mass, leaders in front, across the plain. There can't be more than a few score of soldiers left in charge of the walls. They'll be so terrified, they'll collapse over the top. Everyone who's not for us'll probably try to escape through the north gate. They can go.' He laughed heartily.

'We'll be having a merry time tomorrow night,' he guffawed.

They saw the lights of Rome before the day broke and they made a brief camp in the foothills opposite the city.

'Let me climb up with you to see the lights,' Clodia said. 'I want to see just how unsuspecting Rome appears.'

'They're all sleeping like happy babies,' Martius chortled.

They moved away from the camp, climbing through

152

the trees and undergrowth to the summit of the low hills overlooking the plain.

'You see. Not a murmur. Every soldier forty miles to the south.'

Clodia looked across the black plain to the flickering lights of the city. On the walls sentries would be watching this line of hills, waiting for the first sight of the attack. In the streets and squares, soldiers would be crammed together in their thousands waiting for the gates to open to march out at the startled enemy. But only she knew this.

'This is where you, the other women and the rear guard will watch us from,' Martius told her. 'You'll have to wait an hour before you have the pleasure of joining us – just to make sure there's no unexpected trouble.'

'What trouble could there be? asked Clodia.

'That's right,' Martius said. 'If I had my way, I wouldn't make you wait. But Spartacus is cautious. Never get him to make a false move.'

Clodia felt Martius' arm move around her shoulder. Now was the time, she told herself.

'They say a satisfied man doesn't fight as well as the next,' Martius was saying. 'But I can't see that a quick fuck is going to do me any harm.'

He pulled her over, hands fondling her breasts and she turned onto her back and slipped out of her loincloth.

Martius pulled off his loincloth and she felt his erect penis against her thighs as he rolled onto her.

'Take your sword out; it gets in my way,' she said softly.

'Getting to like it, aren't you, you hot little bitch,' Martius said good-humouredly.

He unsheathed his sword and laid it beside them on the grass.

Clodia put her arms around his neck and kissed him, feeling his moustache on her face as she shot her tongue into his mouth.

She opened her legs and he gave a grunt as he embedded his flesh in her.

Clodia moved her hand down his back, stroking, and then let if fall away, simulating a moan as if in abandon. Her fingers were on the sword at their side. Martius was thrusting into her, grunting heavily. He was oblivious to everything but his senses for the moment.

She moved her hand over the sword, finding the hilt, grasping it. She drew it gently nearer.

Martius gasped with passion as he buried himself completely in her passage.

The gasp became prolonged and grated into silence as the steel ran into his belly.

Trembling, Clodia slithered from under him, pushing him away from her. She looked at him. He was dead. She wiped the blood from her belly and thighs with her loincloth. Quickly she began to pull Martius away from the hill summit, down into the trees. She dragged him over rocks and through bushes for some distance and then let him flop in the scrub. With trembling fingers she began to pull off his tunic. She was frightened, but a sense of urgency impelled her with a cool efficiency.

After fifteen minutes she straightened. In the dark-

154

ness she was a man, dressed in a Roman helmet, tunic and arms. Everything was big for her, but that simply helped to hide her feminine body. Most of the arms and apparel of the horde were stolen. Strange fits were a common sight.

Clodia rubbed dirt into her legs and arms to hide their whiteness. She wished she had some gladiator's greaves. She rubbed dirt and the juice of berries into her face as well. By the time she had done, it was no longer Clodia who walked back towards the camp, but some nondescript soldier, who, if you looked very closely, had a handsome profile and a rather feminine delicacy.

She settled herself against a tree where Martius had left his horse on one flank of the main body. She thanked her stars that he was a lieutenant, keeping himself somewhat away from the body of his men. He was a surly character, too, and few sought his company, few would notice his absence at this tense hour.

Clodia stayed where she was waiting for the dawn. During those moments of time which remained to her, her thoughts went back into the past thinking of all the might-have-beens. Most of her life had been a series of might-have-beens. In spite of her advantages of beauty, wealth and upbringing, she had singularly failed in her personal relationships. She had made mistake after mistake until the final one had reduced her to this. She realised she no longer had any great desire to live. Spartacus was the one man who had really affected her deeply and that result too, had been disastrous. Now she would kill him and probably die herself. She thought this as if she were another person, calmly. Her only fear was that she might not succeed in destroying the Thracian.

When the sun began to rise behind them, the sky to streak pale blue, green and then yellow-silver, and the whole heavens to lift and lighten, Spartacus rode up to the hill summit with Marcellus behind him.

He took a long look at Rome, at the light of morning glowing on its walls, enclosing the seven hills, and then he called to the lieutenants to follow him, to the men to begin the march.

From all directions the leaders galloped to join him. There was a great excitement as the men climbed the hillside and began the descent to the plain.

Spartacus galloped at the head of his few hundred lieutenants. He looked back at the thousands of his men marching across the plain and he felt a thrill quiver inside his calm exterior. What a moment!

Everybody's eyes were glued to the city's walls. Nobody spoke. Nobody noticed the young lieutenant on the flank, whose eyes never left Spartacus.

The gladiator chief reined in his horse to a slower place. He did not want to get too far ahead of his men – although he saw no danger. What resistance could they possibly put up? They might bar the gates while they tried to escape from the northern gate, but it would take him only a few minutes to scale the high walls and open the city to the army behind.

Closer and closer the city came, glorious and never conquered. The plain trembled under the feet of the gladiators' march. The distance lessened.

Spartacus smiled to himself. What would Pompeius say?

And then his smile began to disappear.

The gates of Rome had opened and ranks of horsemen began to gallop out into the sun, arms and armour flashing in the morning rays.

The gladiators' march did not stop. At first Spartacus thought these were the men that remained, coming out on some ridiculous and brave suicidal defence. Then as the numbers swelled and the horsemen split, forming the flanks of a large body of foot soldiers, he realised that he had underestimated.

Even then he thought that perhaps a thousand men had been left to guard the city and the march continued.

But as, in the distance, the thousand men began to spread, turned into a legion, two legions, three legions – and still more poured from the city – he reined in, waved for his men to halt.

As all eyes gazed in startled disbelief at the Roman legions bristling out in defence of city and Empire, the young lieutenant on the flank moved in, weaving between the loose ranks of the lieutenants toward the leader.

The legions advanced. They seemed unending, spreading across the face of the seven hills, a great shining of helmets, a thunderous trampling of feet.

Spartacus sat on his horse, staring grimly into the Roman ranks. Somehow he had been tricked. Crassus would not have sent such a small force to the south, leaving such an enormous one in the city, had he

157

not known what was afoot. Word had gotten to him somehow.

No time now to look for traitors, though.

'What do you think of that?' he said to Marcellus.

'Four or five legions,' Marcellus said grimly. 'Four to one at least.'

'Do we run?' Spartacus asked.

Marcellus looked at his leader. He looked around at the still horde of gladiators and slaves. He looked back at the Romans and drew his sword.

Spartacus laughed.

'We'll still be in Rome tonight,' he said.

Uneasily fingering their weapons, the horde watched their leader. They saw him turn on his horse towards them, a majestic figure. They saw his smile and were warmed by it.

'A gladiator is a better fighter than a Roman any day,' he roared. 'Four heads apiece and it'll be roast duck and wild boar tonight.'

His words carried, were relayed from mouth to mouth across the horde. Every heart was strengthened. What were four Roman heads? Spartacus would claim forty.

A great cheer roared from the throats of his ten thousand men. Spartacus would lead them to victory. He had never failed. He would never fail.

Spartacus waved his sword and the cheer died in ten thousand throats.

From amongst those surrounding him, a figure had suddenly lunged forward, a sword had flashed and Spartacus had fallen downward on his horse, hands hanging limply down across the animal's neck. With his fall, the animal had leapt forward and began to race towards the Roman ranks, carrying the gladiator chief toward the enemy ranks.

Watching from his vantage point at the flank of his troops, Crassus, who had left the command of the first assault to a young aristocrat, had been waiting for Spartacus' death.

He had seen the leader on his black horse, cutting a finer figure than any Roman general. He had heard the cheer. And against all the indication his heart had sunk.

The gladiators and their trainees were a tough bunch who would fight to the death. He had the feeling there would be little left of his beautiful legions to cheer the victory that night.

Had Clodia failed? If only she had got this man out of the way.

And then his heart had spun as he saw the thrust of Clodia's sword and heard the shocked cries with which the spectacle was met. He had tried to see what happened to Clodia. But she was swallowed in the mass. With a sick feeling in the pit of his stomach he was aware she had made no effort to escape.

He had looked back to where the big black horse was racing towards his advancing troops and he saw another horseman racing after it. He shook his head in wonder. The mad courage of these men.

By the time Spartacus' body had slithered from his horse into Roman hands, Marcellus, galloping with a wild fury, was on them. Not a single arrow had been fired at him, so astonished had the marksmen been to see a lone figure bearing down on their 30,000 men.

Marcellus crashed through the Romans cutting them away from Spartacus' body. He fought like ten men, wheeling his bucking horse over the corpse of his leader, covering his prostrate body with the blood of Rome.

Nobody else had moved in the gladiators' ranks. They had sat and stood completely dumbfounded by their leader's death. What hope now?

And when half the horde suddenly lost its head in fury and charged the Romans headlong to avenge their leader, half remained, still slow to join, with only Spartacus' ghost for company.

The gladiators' forces were thus cut in two. Those who attacked fought wildly. Roman blood seemed to run as thick as the Tiber.

Crassus, watching on the flank, wondered what, indeed, would have been the outcome of the day's battle had Spartacus lived, had each of his men fought with the wild vigour the courage of those who attacked.

But of those who still hesitated, some broke and ran for the hills, others put up a bewildered, half-hearted resistance, others again fought as nobly as those who had charged.

But the fight was gone from half the gladiators' army.

At the end of the day, although Roman corpses outnumbered those of their enemy by two to one, Rome was saved, saved with a legion and a half to march triumphantly back.

CHAPTER THIRTEEN

In a mountain clearing in the Appenines, Clodia lay, badly wounded. She was surrounded by a small group of the survivors of the battle.

She had been struck down almost immediately and her horse had bolted. Of those who had fled several had seized her and brought her here to exact full vengeance for their leader's death.

They had soon discovered that she was a woman. Her wound had been staunched and she was stripped to undergo the final indignities.

They kept her for some days, feeding her, submitting her daily to a series of rapes, forcing her with her fading energy to satisfy them.

Then they beat her with whips and the flat of their swords. They turned her over and burned 'S' for Spartacus into her buttocks and then into each of her breasts.

Day after day, Clodia lost consciousness, hoping with her last thought that she would not recover. But day after day she came back to lucidity, her body so mutilated and weak that she was beyond the point where pain seemed to matter. Still they found means of torturing her.

These men became to her like gods. She was completely in their power. If they stopped torturing her for a moment, she felt a great thankfulness for their kindness. When they gave her water or food she worshipped them. When they tortured her again it seemed to her that it was justice and she wished she could die.

Finally, the leader of them pushed her naked body over with his foot one morning.

'It's getting too dangerous for us to stay here,' he told her. 'Do you hear me?'

His voice seemed to come from a long way off. She nodded feebly.

'So we're going to clear out for a few days,' he said. 'But we'll be back for you, because there's one thing more to be done.'

Clodia heard his words and they meant almost nothing to her. What more was there to be done? She knew she had little time to live.

'If it hadn't been for you, Spartacus would have made us all lords in Rome, by now,' the man said savagely. He kicked her and she felt his foot only as a dull, undefined pushing of her flesh.

He scowled down at her for a few seconds.

'Well, now you're going to be strung up,' he said. 'That's what they're doing to those of us they caught and the dead ones.'

Clodia felt no emotion. Her mind was dried up, withered with pain. She was like a dried weed. Nothing could hurt her further.

They strung her up on a tree. They drove stakes through her hands and feet. They left her there alone in the mountains to wait with a great longing for the relief of death.

Marcus Crassus was annoyed. He and he alone had saved Rome from a terrible fate at the hands of the gladiators. Had it not been for him they would all have been slaughtered. And what happened?

Pompeius had landed in the south with stacks of booty and slaves. He had cut off part of the gladiator remnants fleeing to the south and was now the hero of Rome – for almost no reason at all it seemed.

With the security of Pompeius' approach, the Senate had disbanded Crassus' army with nothing but public thanks and a medal for him. And he seemed to be back where he'd started.

Money was his only success.

He strolled now through the forum where the crosses were being made. Bands of slaves were making them – huge crosses of cedar wood. Tall and strong to bear the weight of a man.

An overseer walked among the chained slaves cracking his whip. Sometimes the whip cracked in the air, sometimes it lashed across a naked back and a wretch yelped and stumbled before renewing his work with even greater energy.

Slaves making crosses for slaves who had fought against their fate. That was a salutary lesson for them.

This had been Crassus' idea.

On both sides of the Appian Way he would have them placed. They would stretch from the gates of

Rome to the far distant south, thousands of them, an interminable reminder. A lying, dying and dead monument to Marcus Crassus who had crushed Spartacus and his slave rebellion.

He watched the sweating backs of the slaves toiling. That's where it got them. It would be a long time before there was another such revolt. And they couldn't expect very friendly treatment now, if that was the way they bit the hand that fed them.

'That puts them in their place.'

Crassus turned and gave a guilty start. Lucius Crispus stood beside him.

'It's a pity Spartacus isn't still living to be able to see what's become of his scum,' Crispus added.

Crassus nodded. He wondered how much Crispus knew about it all.

'He was the first to go,' he said.

'Yes. That was a strange thing. Killed by one of his own men, I believe?'

Crassus looked at Crispus thoughtfully.

'Did you see it?' he asked.

'No. Not exactly. It happened so quickly.'

'Yes, it was a strange business,' Crassus agreed.

'That man Spartacus was a strange one,' Crispus went on in discreet, confidential tones.

'Oh? I wondered about him.' Crassus was interested. He wished he'd met the gladiator. He thought of Clodia, of what she had said of the man. He thought of 10,000 men following an ex-slave to their liberty – and then collapsing because suddenly he was with them no more.

'Oh yes, there was something powerful about him.'

164

This was one of the topics of Rome. A topic about which Crispus was in the proud position to know more than anyone else. After all, Spartacus had been his slave. And now that the man was dead he felt he could speak frankly about him – now that the challenge was gone.

'Other people have told me the same thing,' Crassus said.

'Of course he was my chief slave,' Crispus said. 'I saw more of him than anyone else. I never put up with any cheek from him. But I must confess that I never had him whipped. He was not the sort of man you had whipped.'

Crispus paused, wondering if he had made a confession of weakness, if he had said too much. But he could see the interest in Crassus' face.

'They say he was descended from the Thracian princess,' he went on. 'I must say the man had a certain quality. He took natural command of all the slaves of my household.'

'He took natural command of a large portion of the slaves of Italy – much to their present regret,' Crassus added.

'Pretty surprising that he lasted so long and did so much damage, eh?' Crispus said.

'Not really,' Crassus said. 'It was just a question of bad organisation against him.'

'Maybe, maybe,' Crispus admitted. 'But he had a power, he had a power.'

They stood together in the forum watching the slaves toiling in the sun, the sun glinting off the equestrian statue where Clodia had been strung. Crassus

165

began to feel guilty again. He wondered what had happened to Clodia. She had not been among the dead – a surprising fact. And she had not been among the prisoners.

'How is everything with you?' he asked Crispus suddenly.

'Oh, the divorce you mean?' said Crispus, made frank by the unexpected interest. 'Well, as a matter of fact, my wife has disappeared.'

'Oh?'

'Yes. She was living in a wing of the house and it was some time before I realised she was gone. I think she must have fled to the north with some of the others who left. I dare say I'll hear from her in due course.'

'I see,' said Crassus.

'Rather strange, though,' Crispus added with a little shake of his head.

There was another silence and then Crispus looked at Crassus nervously. He hesitated and then said suddenly:

'By the way, I'm giving a banquet in a week or so to celebrate the victory. I do hope you'll be able to come.

CHAPTER FOURTEEN

Another morning rose over Rome. It was the same as all the others, except that there was a certain under-current of excitement.

The shops were crowded, like the streets, with crowds of busy people. Wares were spread onto the roads. Barbers were shaving their customers in full view. Hawkers roamed the streets bartering their sulphur matches for anything they could find in exchange.

Sausage, roast fowl and game were displayed piping hot in pans and ovens by owners of cookshops with an eye to business. Money changers clinked their coins on tables in the market, others pounded gold dust.

In the forum a bear-tamer had his great shaggy animal perform tricks for a large, gaping crowd of idlers. Beggars held out their worn hands for alms, invoking the gods and the natural kindness of the passers-by.

Now and again a horseman would clatter up the narrow streets, a group of laughing soldiers would pass, or perhaps a senator in his red sandals and purple-striped toga would stride thoughtfully toward the law courts.

Everywhere was a torrent of people, sometimes flowing into pools, at others narrowing to a back-street trickle. But always unceasing in noise and movement.

The excitement today was at the approach of Pompeius.

Soon the city would be filled with fresh legions, fresh riches, fresh spectacles, led in triumph by the great general.

Late that afternoon, when Pompeius rode at the head of his men up the Appian Way towards Rome, he passed silently through a vast colonnade of crucified men. Six thousand of them, some living, some dead, hanging in anguished macabre welcome.

And when Crispus went through the gates to join the welcoming crowd, he found a throng at the foot of the cross of the dead Spartacus, the cross nearest to the gates of Rome. He pushed through the crowd, and with a thick feeling of nausea, a mystery was washed away.

As the crowds began to cheer the general's arrival, he found himself gazing at the mutilated, but recognisable body of Clodia, where she had been flung at the foot of Spartacus' cross.

He raised horrified eyes to where the dead man hung.

And it seemed that even in death his power remained.

MADGE BUFORD
Anonymous

My dear Jack:

I have just received your doleful letter and my heart and something else further down yearn to console you. But what can I do for you, way out there in a camp in the Rocky Mountains, with 'not a cunt within a hundred miles' as you say?

Poor Jack, and you so amorous! Would that I had you here, naked in my arms, your ardent kisses covering me from lips to knees, your darling staff resting rigid in my grasp or receiving a caress from parted lips, until ready to burst with its creamy treasures, you would throw me on my back, and breast to breast, belly to belly, tongues hotly thrust into eager, suckling mouths, and arms and legs so interwoven that one could hardly tell – which you, which me – while that stiff staff of yours, that Cyprian sceptre of delight was plunged deeply in my belly. Those soul inspiring thrusts carried such a thrill of ecstasy to my eager cunt, until the acme of all human joy was reached and my thirsty womb drank in the balmy sweets of manly sperm and I bedewed you with my own full measure of ecstatic overflow!

Oh Jack! Dear Jack! would that you were here. But wishes are vain. A thousand miles are between us. But Jack! I remember that the last summer we were together at the seashore you often asked me to tell you of myself, to give you a history of my amorous life; and I put it off until, at last, our pleasure-giving days were rudely cut short by that sudden order from the War Department to join your regiment.

And now, dear Jack! I've the thought that perhaps, while you're away so far, a few pages from my life might give you pleasure, even if the pleasure had to end like Onan's, in the Bible, and the seed be wasted on the barren, western soil, instead of thrilling this yearning crevice of mine that calls out so eagerly to you as I write.

CHAPTER I

I was born in Louisiana among the palms, pelicans, and bayous, where the soft air has an amorous embrace and the half-tropical sun breeds voluptuousness. When I was fourteen my father received a consular appointment in Europe and it was thought best that I should be left in America to complete my education. I can remember no relations of my parents except a middle-aged uncle of my mother's, Uncle John we called him, who was rich but a recluse; going now and then to New Orleans on business, when he would make a formal call, and burying himself at other times in his large plantation, which was isolated in a part of the state distant from any other town.

My parents finally settled on the Convent of the Sacred Heart, in New York, as the place at which I was to complete my education and, taking me there, left me in charge of the sisters, while they sailed for Europe.

I have read much of the illicit intercourse of priests and sisters and novices; but I can recall nothing in this Convent that would raise a blush, even though

173

perhaps I was too young to understand things that, to my present mind, would be suggestive.

Two years passed quietly and in all innocence. I was daily expecting the return of my parents when, one morning, the New York journals were filled with accounts of a great ocean disaster and, in a few years, I knew that I was alone in the world. Not a living soul on earth to look after me, a girl of sixteen.

The good sisters consoled me and treated me with more kindness than ever; but the uncertainty of my future preyed on me and I knew not where to turn. One day, just before the end of the session, I was summoned to the office, and there, with outstretched hand, was Uncle John.

He always seemed so far apart from the rest of us that I had not thought of him. But now he was all kindness and soon made me understand that he was to be my protector and that, for the present at any rate, I was to go live with him at his home.

CHAPTER II

'Beauvoir,' out of the world as it was, charmed me. A one storey house buried among magnolias; a wide piazza all around it, with hammocks and luxurious couches, for here one lives out of doors.

Uncle John told me that the Negro quarters were an eighth of a mile away and that the darkies were not permitted near the house unless summoned. The household servants were Sam and Meg, husband and wife; light-coloured mulattoes, showing the Caucasian features of some white ancestor and each with a form and bearing that would fascinate a sculptor.

I was made at home in a pretty room and Meg assisted me in changing my travelling clothes and robing me in thin garments that left arms and neck bare; meanwhile the kind girl praised my shape and budding charms and I, in turn, laughingly lauded her well-developed figure; making her lift her plump breasts out of her dress and even raise her skirts so that I might see as much of her as she had of me; and so, half naked, I embraced her. For the first time in my life a new sensation seized me, and I know now that voluptuousness was at that moment born within me.

But supper was ready and I, seated opposite Uncle John, ate ravenously and drank some wine, a new thing for me which seemed to add to that unknown sensation that still lingered from Meg's embrace. After supper Uncle John showed me over the house, even to his luxurious bedroom, which was some distance from mine; and then, as I had had a long trip, he called Meg and said that I had better go to bed.

I kissed him, and again that tingling of unknown desires came to me as he pressed me to him; but I was not so overcome that I did not hear him whisper to Meg to come to him as soon as I was in bed. It did not take long with her help, and, wishing me pleasant dreams, she left. I lay in the dark, nervous unsatisfied; wanting something, I knew not what.

I tried to analyse my feelings; find what it was that ailed me; felt of myself to see where the sensation came from. As my roving hand passed over the rounded belly to the tufted mount below, it touched the swelling sentinel of love and my thrilling nerves told me that *here* is what I sought. Feeling the soft crevice, I found, in my gently moving hand, a giver of unknown pleasures, until, my desires teaching my virgin instincts, I threw off the bedclothes, pulled up my night robe, opened wide my legs and, pressing my finger between my cunt's hot lips, soon learned the exquisite delight of rapid friction and lay dissolved in a gulf of languorous pleasure whose meaning I had not yet fathomed. What could it be? My hand and hairy mount were wet with some sticky exudation; my heart beat queerly and I lay in a delicious languor.

I could not make it out and again sought the mysterious grotto, but it did not feel nice, sticky as it was, and I got up and bathed myself. Refreshed, I was about to step into bed when the closing of a door at the other end of the hall made me pause. I heard Uncle John whisper to Meg to come to his room. What for? Could it be anything connected with the delightful phenomena I had just experienced myself? Instinct – the Devil – or I know not what, put it into my virgin mind that it was.

CHAPTER III

The newborn lust within me drove me on. Opening
the door I stepped into the dark corridor and there,
from the open ventilators over the closed door, a
bright light shone, a beacon guiding me to a new
revelation.

Soon I was close to it and could hear Meg and
Uncle John talking; words which I hardly knew the
meaning of. I was on pins and needles. A high backed
chair stood near. Bracing it against the side of the
door I climbed up on its back and my head came to
a level with the open panel; the whole, brightly lighted
room was in full view. Room? Think you I saw aught
of it? No! For, there on the sofa, naked as Adam, sat
Uncle John, leaning back, one hand holding the cigar
he was smoking, the other the erect standard of love.
For the first time I saw the maker of us all, the
emblem of fertility; the one thing on earth without
which a woman would be a useless creation and her
teeming, yearning womb a sterile desert.

Oh, how my eyes glued themselves to his darling
object! How my itching crevice told my innocence

that this was what it yearned for. A column, white as alabaster, long and rigid, crowned as it were, with a jaunty red cap rolling down at the sides like the bars of an arrow; and, at the other end, a great bag as large as my fist and rosy red; while all around this lovely machinery of love, black hair curled in close ringlets, forming a dark background against which the ivory sceptre stood out rampant, the true and only insignia of love.

'Strip, you minx,' he said. 'I've a whole bag full of sperm for you.' And Meg, erect before him, almost with a turn of her hand, stood out in her olive nakedness. Plump arms and legs rounded gracefully; breasts that were veritable tents of love, and swelling belly that seemed to say, 'Come press me.' 'Are you glad to have him back, Meg?' said Uncle John. For all response the darling girl threw herself back on her knees between him, and taking the hairy bag in one hand, with the other she gently grasped the rigid spear moving the white skin up and down, as I could see; for one minute the spry head was covered, the next, exposed and ready to burst. Then the girl sprang to her feet, rushed to the bed, and on her back, her bottom on the edge and with thighs wide open, cried out; 'Come, Master John, come quick! My cunt is on fire! Fuck me! Fuck my cunt!' In an instant I saw the great red head of his cock pressed into the thick curling hair between her legs and, as his hands seized her buttocks, lose itself completely in the fervid crevice.

Lost, yea, for an instant; then out it comes again almost to the head, then in, then out, faster and faster.

'Oh, it's lovely!' cried Meg. 'I'm spending, give it to me!' and, with a quick movement, the panting girl threw her legs around his waist as, with throbbing breasts and heaving belly, I could guess that something, I knew not what, was being shot from his hidden pego – for she cried out to him as she clutched him in the last frantic throes: 'Give me every drop of it!'

I could stand no more; sliding down from the chair I groped my way back to my room and to bed and, in a frenzy of feverish lust, I frigged myself till I fell asleep, languid and exhausted.

CHAPTER IV

With all my lustful yearnings I was frightened at what I had seen and what I had done to myself. For two days I struggled to keep amatory thought out of my head and my hands away from the centre of pleasure. But it was useless. Naked men and women danced before my eyes. I wandered out in the grounds where the poultry were picking their crops full and a stately rooster would make a dive, mount a squawking hen and, with flushed face and puckering slit, I watched their brief spasms of jerks until the cock dismounted and the hen went away shaking her feathers.

One day I was walking along the road and, in the field not fifty feet away from me, a cow was grazing placidly. Suddenly I heard a low bellowing and, across the field, I saw a bull jump the fence and, with a mad rush, make for the cow, who, seeing him coming, turned to run. But it was too late. With a wild rush the lustful animal sprang forward; for an instant I saw him raised on his hind legs, that monstrous instrument of his sticking out like a mast from his belly; then down he came upon the cow's back, his forelegs clutching her sides and his panting flanks working like the piston rod of a steam engine until, the discharge coming, his speed lessened and I felt such that he was experiencing the same languor that I had felt the night I saw Uncle John and Meg together.

The sight fired me: I forgot my good resolutions and, rushing to a little clump of trees, I pulled up my skirts and with eager hand, rubbed the itching of my carnal cavity until the ecstasy of a copious discharge left me limp.

From that day to this I have not checked my amorous desires when a person and place suited, and prudery alone stood in the way.

That night, as Uncle John kissed me goodnight, I saw his eyes sparkle as they looked down upon the blossoming bubbies which my frock but partly hid; the arms around my waist dropped down and, with a spasmodic motion, he pressed my buttocks until we were so close together that I thought that I felt a hard substance in his breeches print itself against my belly. An instant thus, and releasing me he hastened to his room and I to mine.

I was wild; I stripped to my chemise and, barefooted, stole along the hall, mounted my chair and, again, through the fanlight, saw the heaven I yearned for.

With gently frigging hands between my legs, I saw him undress until, naked, he stood there, his lovely cock bolt upright against his belly. He took it in his hand and, the better to see it, I made a movement on my perch and – well – the next I knew I was on my back on the floor.

CHAPTER V

There, half stunned, ashamed, I lay a moment and before I could collect myself and fly, the door opened wide, the light streamed full upon my almost naked person and Uncle John stood over me.

I simply covered my face with my hands and lay there panting. In an instant I was lifted in his strong arms, one around my naked waist and the other hand pressed to my hairy nest.

In an instant my chemise was torn away and I lay naked in his lap, his eyes burning into mine, his hands wandering from my firm globes over my swelling belly and nestling between my legs, and his fingers penetrating the lips of love. 'So – so – Miss Madge, you wanted to see what a man looked like, did you? So you shall. Give yourself up to it, dear!'

His hot lips were pressed to mine, his tongue thrust hotly in and then my nipples were his prey and his rapture-giving hand soon brought my heaving thighs to a climax of enjoyment.

'Oh!' I cried, throwing my arms around his neck. 'This is heaven!' 'Yes, my dear girl for you; but I'm in hell! Just see!' Lifting me up and standing by my side, he took my hand and carried it to his over-wrought pego. Oh! the first touch of that velvety truncheon! The quick grasp! – and then, his hand guided mine in the rapid, electric moving of the flexible skin upon the fixed flesh beneath – his buttocks working, his arm clutching me closely to him! 'Go on! go on!' he cried. 'Watch it Madge, watch it shoot!' I felt his prick swell larger and larger in my grasp; his lips poured ravishing kisses on every spot of flesh he could reach and then – high in the air flew great drops of thick milky sperm-drops coming so fast that they seemed to be a stream of love lava.

Slowly the spasm quieted, and seizing me in his arms, he threw me flat on the bed and rolled on top of me, breast to breast, belly to belly, open mouth to open mouth, breathing into each other; tongue sucking, each of his hands grasping a plump cheek of my buttocks and his fallen but lusty prick and balls rubbing against my sensitive cunt until, with a convulsive clutch, with arms and legs around him, I poured down my oblation to the god of love.

As I lay languishing he seized my hand and put his stiffened pego in its grasp, asking me if I did not want to examine it, and, as I held it upright, moving the soft skin gently up and down or weighing in my hand the heavy bag of love elixer, he told me all about it – why it stiffened, how it broke its way into the virgin slit, and sowed the seeds from which we all grow. He told me of the danger of indiscreet commerce in this artificial and conventional world. But he told me also, the many ways that lustful pleasure could be had with

185

perfect safety. His glowing language and gentle but hot caresses re-illuminated the fires within me and I pressed my ardent mount convulsively to his hand. 'You want more do you?' he cried. 'Yes, dear John, give me more. I'm hotter than ever!' Flat on his back, his head and shoulders raised on a pillow, he lifted me up, straddled me across him, and, pulling me towards his face kissed my navel, belly, and thighs. Then his hot lips sought my eager cunt; his tongue gently tickled the sensitive membrane until squirming and wriggling from its embraces, I gave a cry of pleasure. Thrusting his elongated tongue deep into my burning slit, he worked it in and out, holding me tightly to his face, until my whole body seemed to dissolve itself in a blissful overflow and go gushing down to meet his lascivious embraces.

He held me thus for a moment, weltering in my enjoyment, then seizing me, he laid me on my back against the pillows straddled across my chest – 'Make a cunt of your titties,' he cried, and as his proud prick pressed against my breasts, I squeezed my plump globes around it and held it tightly. His buttocks began to work and I had the lovely spectacle, close to my eyes, of his swelling staff, now all in view; then only its ruby head shining between my snowy bubbies – when, ready to spend, he cried: 'Now watch it!' and the great jets of cloudy essence flew high over my head, hit my cheek, fell in a copious shower on shoulder, arm and breast until, seizing my head, he raised me up – 'Suck it!' he cried. 'Make a cunt of your mouth; squeeze my balls! That's it – roll your tongue around it! That's good – suck harder; swallow

186

every drop I've got,' until breathless, I threw myself back and he, springing up, brought my thighs to the edge of the bed. Kneeling, holding my buttocks firmly in his grasp, he brought down again my ever ready balm with lightning working tongue.

He would not let me stay longer, but bathing me with refreshing cologne, took me in his arms and carried me to bed, making me promise not to touch my touchy tid-bit, but go straight to sleep. But, before he left my bedside I threw my arms around his hips and rained a dozen kisses on the now fallen and flabby idol of my desires.

CHAPTER VI

The next day he told me how debilitating and injurious it was to yield to love too much, especially in one so young; but he promised me that, on the morrow, he would again taste pleasure.

The morrow came. He ordered the horses saddled and we had a bracing gallop through the woods, returning with blood pounding healthfully through our veins and ravenously hungry. We ate heartily and two glasses of old wine made my whole body tingle with voluptuous desires.

'How demure and modest you look in that riding habit,' said he. 'I don't feel so,' I answered and, unbuttoning my waist with both hands, I held up to him my stiff-nippled titties. 'How lovely!' he cried. 'Now let me see the other hill, the shaded mount of Venus.' And, jumping to my feet, I pulled the long, modest, black riding habit up to my waist and exposed to his ardent eyes my palpitating belly. He was on his feet in an instant, and tearing open his trousers pointed his darling dart lustfully at me across the table. 'Fill your glass!' he cried. 'Fill it full. Drink it

all; you to this branch of coral – I, to that rosy crevice.'
Draining the glasses – the lively wine spread still more
ardent fires in our veins.

'Run!' he cried. 'Lift your clothes as high as they
will go and run ahead of me to my room.' And,
snatching up my skirts I threw them over my shoulder
and ran at full speed along the hall; throwing myself,
panting, upon the bed and he on me. His stiff cock
rubbed against my belly and against my hairy mount;
then, turning me upon my stomach, he pressed it
against my plump backsides and, as it nestled cosily
between the rounded cheeks, he rubbed it there, while
his eager hand sought out my raging slit, and cock
and hand moving in unison, we both went off together
in delightful ecstasy.

Recovering, we stripped and, making me stand on
a sofa with one leg lifted on his arm, he washed away
the sticky overflow, bathed me with perfume and,
giving my mount a parting kiss, I jumped down and
he took my place while I, in turn, bathed him and
paid him back with kisses on his humble cock.

Going to a bookcase he brought out a volume, and
taking me on his lap, he opened it. Oh, such pictures!
Naked men and women coupled together in every
conceivable way! All the forms and fashions of lust
which the lecherous imagination of centuries have
invented and practised; what a revelation it was! My
hand instinctively sought his prick while, with one
arm under my bottom, his fingers stroked my pussy.
Each page was new and provocative. We were nearing
the need for action, when, skipping a number of pages,
he opened to a picture of a lovely girl upon her side

and a handsome man in front of her, his head buried between her thighs and her lustful mouth filled with his inflamed pego. 'How splendid!' I cried. 'Both can enjoy it at once,' and springing up, I threw myself prone upon the soft crimson rug on the floor. In a moment he was beside me, his lips covering my burning slit, his tongue tickling and thrusting, while my eager mouth closed tightly on his lovely, ruby headed spear; kissing, tongue-rolling, bag squeezing, buttock clutching − sucking, till the thick sperm bathed our mouths, throats and was gulped down to seethe in lustful satisfaction in our bellies.

We lay ten minutes thus lost in delicious lassitude. Don't say that sucking the carnal parts is disgusting! Why is not a prick or cunt as clean and wholesome to kiss and taste as a mouth? Why, if I will let a cock play tag in my belly, should I be squeamish if he wants to enjoy the contact of lips and tongue? Both openings are lined with the same membrane and one is as wholesome as the other.

Let the prude pucker only with her slit if she chooses; but for me my lover is welcome to all the holes I've got.

John filled a goblet with wine and, as I still lay panting on the floor, handed it to me and, drinking half, he finished it. Then, getting upon the bed, he filled it again and made me bring my buttocks to the edge of the bed, prop myself up on a pillow, stretch my thighs wide-open and round up my belly. He then poured the whole glassful down the crevice of my slit, his mouth catching it below and his lips and tongue licking up the last drops. Then, again filling the goblet, he gave it to me and, kneeling before me, I washed and bathed his fallen cunt tickler in the wine and then drank all of it – ending by kissing away the drops that hung from his staff or glistened on the curly hair or swollen testicles.

Then he went and got the picture book which we had not finished, and reclining against the pillows, he seated me between his thighs, his prick pressed against my bottom and my legs spread out between his.

Smutty pictures are the true arrows of Venus. Half the women in the world are awkward in attempting lust; backward in lewd variety even when they are willing and anxious to please. But they are imitative and a picture from life will give them a carnal wrinkle.

Turning over the leaves of this concupiscent gallery of lecherous attitudes we came to one which I did not understand. A woman lying belly down across the waist high arm of a sofa, her magnificent bum showing its sumptuous and luxurious richness of flesh in bold prominence; behind her a man had his long and slender staff embedded – where? Not in her slit; it's too far back for that. 'What a poor drawing!' I said. 'Her quim is not there, it's further front.' John laughed. 'Don't you know my dear, that every woman has two openings down there? That fellow has his prick in her cul: in plain English, in her ass-hole. It's tight and fits a cock snugly and some men lust for that more than for the regular channel.'

'How funny,' I said. 'I never dreamed of such a thing.' And as I spoke, John's stiffened prick stuck between the broad cheeks of my buttocks.

191

I looked up into his face. 'Do you want to?' I asked. He did not answer, but, jumping up, thrust his pego into my face. 'Wet it with your mouth,' he cried, 'so that it will slide easier.' And I obeyed, spreading the saliva over end and sides, so that when he took it out, it glistened with moisture. Lifting me up he led me to the sofa and, pushing me over the cushioned arm, had my broad buttocks boldly offered to his attack. Quickly he penetrated my cul; slowly like a new glove the yielding sides made room for its rigid visitor. It smarted, but I did not wince. I clutched the sofa and braced myself to meet his new and bolder storming of my person. What was the smart to the novelty of these new sensations? And when, passing his hand in front, he fingered my clitoris, I cried out: 'Don't mind me; put it in all the way. I don't mind the hurt,' and with feelings wound up to the fullest tension of lustful activity by the novel scabbard in which his sword was sheathed, he urged it boldly in almost to the hilt. Keeping time with fucking cock and frigging hand, I soon felt the swelling forerunner of dissolving bliss and, with wanton, wriggling thighs, spent freely in his hand while my stretched cul received the easing balm of his discharge.

CHAPTER VII

Twice a week our naked bodies worshipped in the temple of Venus and Priapus. On other days we were so simply affectionate, just a man and a woman; avoiding all provocation and storing up the amorous juices and energy that made us fresh and eager for our holiday of lasciviousness.

I often wondered if Meg and Sam knew what was going on. If they did they made no sign – and as John (I had dropped the Uncle after our first bare-bellied bout) said nothing about them I kept silent.

A rainy Sunday came, John and I had passed the morning in the library, he with a bundle of journals which had just arrived and I with a sentimental novel that made me yawn. Presently it was dinner time and chatting pleasantly, I noticed that John filled my glass with wine more freely than usual. Soon I felt its exciting effects, felt them most acutely down in that touchy little crevice that was palpitating under the tablecloth. But I had promised not to seek pleasure except on the regular days and I kept silent.

'Madge,' he said, 'this is my birthday.'

'Oh! I wish I had known it before, I would have given you a present!' Then, with flushed face, my pouting slit prompting me, I jumped up, ran to his side and pulling my dress up to my waist, cried out: 'Dear John, won't you take this? Take my virginity, I'm dying to give it to you.'

'You darling girl!' he said, kissing my belly and mount. 'I know that you would give to me freely; and you know that no pleasure on earth would be as great to me as piercing your virgin womb. But think, Madge! You are so fresh, and some day a handsome lover will come along and you and he will marry; not until then must the dear little slit of yours be opened. No, Madge, not that. But we will celebrate the day with a revel of voluptuousness.'

He filled another glass of wine and, drinking half, made me finish it. Then, ringing the bell, Meg appeared. 'Take her to my room,' he said, and the lively girl, putting her arm around me, danced with me to his room. 'What it is, Meg? What does it mean?' She would not answer, but, leading me into a small room adjoining my uncle's, tore off every stitch of clothes she had on and then did the same to me and, naked as we were, dragged me into John's room, which was brilliantly lighted and in the centre of which a narrow couch was standing, a convenient altar for sacrificing to Venus.

Leading me up to a mirror we gazed upon the reflections of our naked forms, one rosy-brown, the other rosy-white. 'I guess that picture will stiffen things,' she said, and, as she spoke, we heard the door open and there, facing us, stood John, naked, his lance

194

at rest, and, beside him, Sam, his brown, muscular body bare and his magnificent pego standing bolt upright against his belly.

'Oh, I'm wild!' I cried, rushing into John's arms. 'Give relief quick!' He seized me, and laid me flat on the altar. 'Give her a tongue fuck, Sam.' And, in an instant, the eager mulatto was on his knees before me pressing my thighs open to their widest extent; and then, with long, pointed tongue, darting thrust on thrust into my widely stretched slit and with thick, lecherous lips, caressed the sensitive convolutions. Oh, the flashes of almost agonising pleasure that shot through me! And when the crisis came I fairly shrieked as I spent. The three of them watched me wriggling and heaving for a moment. Then John, seizing Meg, threw her across me and said: 'Now, Madge, you can see what a real fuck is like!' and for response I seized his cock and guided it into her slit. 'Oh, how delicious that must be!' I shrieked. 'It is,' cried Meg, 'give it to me harder!' and, like a horse in the stretch of a race track, John spurted. 'How I feel it!' she cried, 'squeeze his balls.' And I did, and from a wild dance to heave and thrust, they quieted down to a gentler throbbing.

'Jolly! I can't wait,' yelled Sam, holding up his burning rod. And John, taking his melting poker out of Meg's furnace, seized my hand and made me, myself, guide Sam's enormous cock into Meg's slippery slit. He was wound up and wasted no time on gentle heaves, but clutching her bottom in his hands, made his thrusts so hard and fast that the girl yelled out, 'He'll knock a hole through me.' But he kept on and in a second, cried: 'There, you bitch, you whore, take that!' And, knowing that he was spending, I squeezed his testicles, but, overcome with my emotions, I fell back on the floor and eagerly clutched my slit in my hands. But John snatched it away and cried out: 'Come, you rascal. Come, do what you like with this smutty virgin. Put your tongue in her and make her suck that big cock of yours.' 'You mean it?' cried Sam, drawing his still rampant rod out of Meg's pickling tub. But he did not wait for an answer. Like a wild animal he pounced upon me, stretching my thighs as wide as they would go and stuck his tongue deep into my coral slit; while I, frantic with lust, threw myself on his belly and seizing his still magnificent erection, sucked away every drop of sperm that was still oozing from that great rod that filled my mouth completely, until out of breath, we lay panting, our heads resting on the inside of each other's thighs, our hands gently soothing the exhausted warriors of love.

John threw himself down beside us and watched with gloating eyes, our still heaving flanks. But Meg's lustful emotions were calling loudly for assuagement. With a bound she sprang to the mantlepiece, snatched a large candle from its socket and, coming to where we three lay in a huge jumble together, she planted a foot on each side of our outstretched bodies and, in full view of our eyes, which were fixed upon her extended crevice, she plunged the candle deep into its depths, and with deft and rapid motions of her agile hand diddled herself until, exhausted, she staggered to the bed and threw herself on her back, the candle almost lost to sight.

She put her hand down to remove it, but it was in so far and so slippery that she could not get hold of it. 'Oh dear, I can't get it out!' she cried. 'Wouldn't it be awful if I was plugged up for good.' I ran to help her, but my fingers could gain no purchase on the candle's sperm-bathed sides: so, kneeling down, I bade her open her legs to the utmost and, pressing my jaws close to her slit, I managed to catch the slippery dildo with my teeth and so draw it out.

We all laughed at this episode and Meg and I stood up and gazed down upon our two stalwart stallions still stretched upon the floor, side by side, but heads to feet. 'Oh, she cried. 'See them feeling at each other,' and so they were, each handling the other's cock. 'Go on!' she cried. 'All's fair in lust; I'm dying to see them suck each other!' 'We will,' said John, 'but go and get those whips on the shelf and birch our buttocks while we taste the sweets of each other's nuts.'

Wrought up, as we were by this ultra-exciting if outrageous conjuncture, we each seized a whip and, as those stalwarts rolled upon their sides and with lustful lips seized each other's cocks, Meg let fall her whip upon the broad buttocks of her husband while I rained tingling blows upon John's white backsides, until it turned as rosy as my nipples.

It was disgusting – say you – perhaps it was. But to us, frenzied and drunk with all the lechery that four votaries of wantonness can, when untrammelled by prejudices, pour into each other's souls – it lost its forbidding aspects and seemed but one step further in the drama we so loved to act: *Lust a l'outrance*.

CHAPTER VIII

Time passed. Anxious to run no risks with my health, John kept me limited to weekly revels; and I was obliged at other times to recall the pleasures that had passed, or dream of what would happen when next we gave ourselves to the delightful play.

One morning John found a letter which seemed to engross him more than the others. 'Well, Madge! we are going to have a visitor.' 'Oh, I hope not!' I said involuntarily. 'It's too nice now, I hate strangers.' 'It can't be helped. His name is Ralph Brown, the son of my first love. His mother and I, when a little older than you are now, met and in a week we were secretly betrothed. I was summoned away on business. The last night before I left we wandered down to the shore and, seated alone there on the sand in the bright moonlight, we threw off all restraint.

'The dear girl forgot all her former modesty and did not chide me as I strained her to my breast and rained hot kisses upon her lips and shoulders. 'I am all yours,' she cried. But, wiser than to do what would be sorrow to her, I palpitated her sweet breasts and, both urged on by the same desire, I threw myself upon her panting form and, raising her skirts, my eager belly was pressed naked to hers and each, for the first time, tasted the ultimate pleasure of life; but without my penetrating her virgin bower. Again and again did we give ourselves up to these outward libations and all the pleasures that roving, eager hands could yield. I never saw her after that night. She married and they are both dead. When I was in Europe and she dying, she wote me her last message: how she had loved me better than any other; and asking me to watch over her son. It is this son who is coming to see us. I found a good business for him in New York and, whenever he has a vacation he comes to see me. He will be here tomorrow and stay a fortnight.'

He paused, and, looking at me sharply: 'Why Madge, you don't seem to like the idea of his coming!' 'Oh, John!' I cried, throwing my arms around his neck and kissing him, 'if you are pleased, I ought to be, but – ' 'But what?' 'Oh, we seem so happy and now we will have to be – be so very proper.' 'Oh ho, you minx!' he laughed and, thrusting his hand under my clothes took hold of my brush. 'This is what you mean, isn't it?' 'Yes, John, I shall miss it dreadfully. It's awful to be cold and proper after we have passed so many pleasant days, hot and improper.' 'At any rate, let us make hay while the sun shines!'

I was sitting on his knees; stooping, he grasped one of my ankles and, laughing, raised it high in the air, almost upsetting me, and brought it down on the other side. I found myself straddled across his legs.

'Now, my dear little cock pleaser, strip, and let me have a little hot buff and fur to pump sperm for me.' As he held a plump thigh on each side of him, I tore off my garments and, in a minute, sat there stark naked.

Then he made me first put one leg and then the other on his shoulder. Taking off my shoes and lifting me up, he pressed my hairy mount to his face and thrust his tongue in and out of my slit. Then he sat me on a sofa and, standing between my thighs, made me unbutton his trousers and take them off, while he tore off his coat and shirt. Naked, he stood before me, his lovely pego staring me right in the face. I laid it between my bubbies, fondled its soft coat, squeezed the wrinkled storehouse of love and, beginning at the foot of the tower, kissed with open lips and caressing tongue each inch of its tall stature, until the ruby head slipped boldly into my mouth.

'You're wetting it!' he cried, and, indeed, this big mouthful did cause the saliva to secrete. 'I'll be wet myself between my legs in a minute,' I cried. 'Yes, and your cul will be the wettest of all!' he cried, and, lifting me up, he placed me on my knees on the bed, brought his prick to the tight channel and, regardless of my squirming 'Oh's' drove it in and, tickling my nipples with one hand, he rubbed my fervid slit with the other until the flood gates were opened and I was inundated with the essence of love; his behind, mine in front. Soon he rolled over on his back: 'Come, glue your sticky slit to my mouth.' And mounting across his face, he smothered his head between my thighs, while I, throwing myself forward, seized his sperm

200

covered pintle in my mouth and sucked it until, breathless, I rolled over on my back and gave a long drawn cry of satisfied lechery.

CHAPTER IX

Several days later I was walking on the road, when a natural need made itself felt: I wanted to make water. Again, why say: 'Make water,' why not 'piss,' right out? Going to the side of the road, I gathered my clothes up to my waist and, squatting down, a pretty little golden puddle glistened in the sun. Rising erect and still holding my skirts up to my navel, I heard a step crackle on the dry road and, looking up, there before me stood a handsome man, seemingly in the twenties, with flashing eyes surveying my naked charms. I was spellbound, but in an instant he had his arms around my waist and a hand groping my moist mount. 'Oh ho!' said he, 'you're a virgin, are you? Well! you shall have it outside, if not in.' And pushing me back upon a mound of grassy sward, he stood between my legs and, opening his breeches, I had one glimpse of his lovely white pego as he threw himself upon me, raining kisses on my lips, his hot staff and crisp balls delighting with quick friction my hot slit.

Of course I struggled, squirmed, kicked, and called

him all sorts of names, until I felt the climax approaching to both and as I spent and could feel his sperm jetting all over my belly, I had to shut my eyes and press tight my lips to keep from showing the pleasure I was enjoying.

Springing up, he stepped back to gloat over the sight of my panting charms. With a bound I was on my feet and gathering up my dress, I sprang away and ran across the field. He followed for a moment, but soon gave it up and, calling to me: 'We'll meet again, you dear,' he resumed his route along the road. I hastened home and was just beginning to tell Uncle John of my adventure when a knock came, and Meg said that a gentleman wanted to see John.

CHAPTER X

Going to my room, a bath and change of dress somewhat quieted my feelings aroused by that bold
stranger, and by the time that Meg came into the
room to tell me that John and his guest were waiting
to go to dinner, I was ready to join them, looking like
a modest maiden whom a smutty word would send
into convulsions.

'Ralph – this is Madge.' That was the introduction,
and as I looked up at him, I beheld the bold ravisher
who, an hour before, had stared lustfully into my eyes
while his hot sperm shot all over my belly. My heart
stood still and I could hardly bow in answer to his
salute, and I sank into my chair.

Fortunately, the two men had much to say to each
other and I had time to gain my composure, only to
have it routed again when I glanced up and found his
eyes fixed upon me with the same vivid passion that
had kindled my amorous soul when lying on the grass
at his lustful mercy.

For three days I had no chance to be confidential
with John, nor was I alone with Ralph for a minute.

I avoided him. But his image was always before me. On the third day, as I was going to bed. Meg stole into my room. 'Oh, Miss Madge! You ought to have seen him!' 'Seen who?' I asked. 'Our visitor,' she said, 'as I came along the hall the light was bright in his room and I couldn't help peeking through the key-hole. There he was facing the door and pulling his shirt over his head; all bare, and that lovely fresh cock of his standing stiff against his belly. I must frig myself, Miss!' And the dear girl threw herself back upon the sofa and, with her hand, rubbed the excited slit until, by her motions and glowing face, I saw that nature had come to her relief.

Of course I was on fire and, when she came to the bed and gazing down upon me, said, 'Oh, wouldn't you and he make a lovely couple in bed together doing the double-backed beast in your holiday clothes?' I could stand it no longer. Pushing my naked thighs to the edge of the bed, I cried out to her to give me relief; and the kind wench soon had me thrilled with her nimble tongue and then, tucking me into bed, she left me to dream that I was part of the double-backed beast she spoke of.

I kept in my room as much as possible for I felt so awkward when I caught those bold glances of our visitor, though his manner towards me was always coldly respectful.

On the fourth day John went over to the farm-hands' quarters and I thought that Ralph had gone with him. So, going to the library, I threw myself on a sofa with a book when, from the window curtains, stepped Ralph and, standing in the middle of the floor with folded arms, he said: 'Madge, I love you and want to marry you, will you have me?' My heart was in my mouth. 'No, no!' I cried. 'I cannot – never,' and jumping to my feet, I fled to my room and threw myself sobbing, on the bed.

Did I regret the amorous dalliance with Uncle John that now arose as a barrier to the enjoyment of my new flame? No – and yet I only knew that I was miserable. I must have lain there an hour with my heart torn with conflicting emotions when I heard the door of my room pushed open and, starting up, I beheld my new lover standing, naked, with folded arms, in the middle of the room. 'Madge, John has told me all. Tomorrow we will marry. I want you to come and give yourself to me now.'

Oh, the revulsion of feeling! What cared I for weddings! We loved! I sprang up and with trembling hands loosed my few garments and let them drop to the floor, then started towards him with outstretched arms. He eluded me. 'I want to feast my eyes for the last time upon my hot little virgin,' he said. But his eager lust was not to be delayed and, seizing me in his arms, raining kisses on every part of my naked body which I returned with equal fervour, he laid me on the bed and knelt beween my open legs.

'What do you want, Madge?' 'I want you to make a woman of me, burst my virginity with that dear spear of yours. I shan't mind the hurt.' And he was on me, his red lance aimed straight between my cunt's hot lips and forcing its way, little by little, till driven reckless by his sensations, 'Brace yourself, Madge!' and, holding my bottom tightly, his iron rod burst into the useless prison and, wriggling, panting, his magnificent cock was buried to the hilt in my slit and, powerless to wait longer, his swift motion soon brought the voluptuous acme and my smarting slit was soothed by his seething sperm.

Oh, the delicious agony of the moment – pain and pleasure mixed, but the pleasure all conquering! Oh, the languid ecstasy of lying there with his dear form pressed on breast and belly!

And, when our breath returned and he had made needed ablutions, we lay reclining side by side, how fervid the sensation of roving kiss and hand; the avidity of each to explore all the charms we had for each other. My hand had not long caressed his dear hymen breaker before its proud head was lifted again.

'Madge,' he cried, lifting me up on my knees, my hairy, gaping slit before his eyes, 'the second erection to enter here will not be mine. Think how your Uncle John must be suffering. Go and give him the only thing you kept from him.' 'No, no, Ralph. I'm yours now!' 'Madge, jealousy is the cause of half the unhappiness in married life. I'll swear on this dear cunt, and you on my stiff prick, that each will love the other more than all else on earth, but that each shall take pleasure at other founts; knowing that we love each other so well that these wanton excursions will serve but as a stimulant to our mutual pleasures. I kiss the book,' he said, as he pressed his lips and tongue against my slit. Then, springing up – 'Now you kiss, too!' and he held the rosy headed rod to receive my ardent lips.

CHAPTER XI

'Come,' he said, and leading me to John's door, Ralph opened it and, pushing me in, closed it softly. I advance quietly to the head of the bed where I had so often tasted nameless sweets, and gazed down upon John's nude form, stretched there on his back, his mind filled no doubt with vivid pictures of the voluptuous drama being enacted at the other end of the hall and holding the inflamed arrow of love erect in his hand.

'Ralph sent me, John. He has ravished my virginity and swears that he won't fuck me again until your sperm mixes with his in my belly.' 'You darling girl! Do you mean it?' and wildly seizing me in his arms he threw me flat on my back and, kneeling between my thighs I grasped his dear old cock in my hand and, myself, guided it to my newly opened quiver.

Oh, that rapture giving tongue, fucking my mouth; that stiff strong prick fucking my cunt; that thrilling flood of boiling sperm shooting at last into its proper channel and now, for the first time, sending bliss to my innermost vitals. How we squirmed and twisted

208

in our lustful embrace and how happy and content we lay, regaining our breath, till a voice at our side roused us.

'Did you enjoy it?' and looking up, there stood Ralph in all his naked, manly beauty, his pego up in arms. Quickly raising himself, John held out his hand, which Ralph grasped, while I, seizing them both, pressed them, joined together, to my happy slit. Then I sprang up and with an arm around each manly form I kissed first one, then the other, and exclaimed: 'Oh! how happy I am with two such lovers!' 'Let us look at ourselves,' said John, and, with encircling arms, we ran up to the mirror and gazed with lustful eyes on the splendid picture of our naked charms.

'On your knees and worship Priapus,' said Ralph. As I dropped on my knees, he turned my head to John's pego, which I quickly seized in my mouth, and which quickly stiffened; and then, with eager lips, I turned to kiss the rampant rooster that had just crowed for the first time – in my virgin belly.

Raising me, they made me stand straddled on two chairs and, each in turn, standing under my crotch, thrust his tongue into my quiver. 'This is too much, how I wish I had two cunts, so as to have both fuck me at once!' 'You know you have!' said John, 'didn't I take your "maiden-behind" and Ralph your maidenhead?' 'Let's put both in at once!' cried Ralph and, making me stoop, his rigid rod was soon engulfed in my excited slit, when John, lifting up my legs, crossed them tightly around Ralph's waist and I was suspended there – hung upon a peg, as it were – while

John, pointing his spear against my well-stretched bottom, pierced me to the hilt.

Oh! The wild shouts of agonising rapture that deluged me as those two lusty darts of love were driven with simultaneous thrusts into my quivering body, and as the double dose of sperm was shot, like molten lead, into me, I shrieked aloud till Ralph's nimble tongue, with prick-like stiffness, was urged into my cunt-like mouth and I sucked it, as my contracting slit and cul sucked from their pricks the last lovely drops of sperm.

I almost fainted as they laid me on the bed; but a good stiff horn of whisky poured down my throat revived me, and bathed with spirits, I soon lay happy across Ralph's lap on the sofa while John, lighting a cigar, sat naked in an easy chair opposite us and told us smutty incidents in his life.

CHAPTER XII

Meg and Sam kept in the background since Ralph appeared. But I had not forgotten them. One day, after we had rested after the effects of our razzle-dazzle, John was away and Ralph, as we left the table, lit his cigar and, groping me, told me to go to my room and strip and, as soon as he finished smoking, he would come and we would have a nice, quiet little diddle all by ourselves.

I pressed the bulging balls in his breeches and going to my room, threw myself naked on the bed to wait for him. Just then Meg passed the door and I called her in. I had been too busy with my own slit and Ralph's and John's dear cocks to think of her or Sam, but, as she stood by the bed, I sprang up and embraced her. 'Oh Meg, forgive me! We've been so busy with ourselves. Come strip, get into bed with me and when Ralph comes, I'll make him give you a taste of his old gentleman.' 'No, no, Miss Madge, he is all yours!' But I jumped up and commenced tearing off her clothes.

211

Just as I, standing upon the bed, was pulling her chemise over her head, Ralph entered.

'See how two girls can enjoy each other!' I cried, and I threw the wench on the bed and, with mouths glued to each other's slits, we gave him a lively duet of tongue thrusting. While watching us he stripped and, as we lay languidly, side by side, he approached and examined my dusky bed-fellow. 'What a nice, plump little brown Venus it is?' he said, as his hands roved over her. 'Leave me alone,' she said, 'you belong to Miss Madge.'

But I took Ralph's prick in my hand and held it up, rigid and fierce: 'Do you mean to tell me you don't want a taste of his?' I asked. 'Oh, I do, Miss. I do. My slit's hot now!'

'Get on your knees,' I cried, 'so that I can see the whole race up and down your hairy place!' and the lusty wench did as I told her, and, giving Ralph's rooster a parting kiss, I pointed it for her centre of attraction and gave myself up to the delightful spectacle of their lusty working bung and spigot, and, when Meg's well-filled belly rolled, squirming, upon the bed, I clasped Ralph's loins in my hands and took the fallen monarch in my mouth, sucking into me the last drop.

'One of you must tongue tickle me, quick!' I cried. 'Hold on!' said Ralph, snatching away his hand which I had clasped against my slit. 'Where's that robust husband of yours, Meg? Go and fetch him and tell him there's a lady here who wants the use of his cock for a few minutes.' 'Shall I Miss?' cried the delighted wench, spring to her feet. 'Hurry up!' said Ralph, and he gave her plump backside a resounding smack with his hand as the girl sprang naked out of the door.

'Oh, Ralph! do you really want me to let that black man fuck me?' I asked. 'I know you have let him kiss my slit and suck it, and I've kissed him too and twice he went off in my mouth; but, if he fucks me straight, I might have a brown baby.' Ralph laughed aloud. 'Babies or not,' he cried, 'I'm going to see that big muscular fellow fuck you right up to the handle,' and he threw himself on the bed and pulled me down, with my rump on the edge, tickling my nipples and clitoris as I lay across him.

A moment thus and, in the doorway, appeared the sprightly wench, and beside her, the magnificently muscular and manly form of Sam. He was a little bashful at this sudden introduction into such company, but the royal prick that the wench held in her hand showed how excited his passions were.

'See, Miss!' cried she, 'isn't it a whopper?' 'Walk up to the captain's office and settle!' cried Ralph. And, as Sam advanced and stood between my thighs I lost all my fears and took the splendid specimen of virility in my hand. 'What a monster he is!' I cried. 'He's grown bigger than ever!' 'Jolly, Miss,' said Meg, 'he's had lots of exercise since you and Massa John and Massa Ralph have been fucking and sucking each other all over the house. We had to peep in sometimes and see you three fooling with each other, and this rascal when you all came to the going off point, would make me get down on my knees and suck him while he watched you three wriggling.' 'You wicked peeper!' I cried. 'I'll pay you for that! Go and get that whip

213

Meg, and thrash his backsides.' And I guided his immmense prick between the lips of my slit and threw myself back, panting, to taste this luscious morsel.

'Quat her just as you would Meg!' cried Ralph, and seizing my bum the lusty gentleman thrust that soul-satisfying shaft of his plump rod up to the hilt. 'Oh, it's splendid! It's a splitter, don't spare me, it's so lovely! Don't hold back! That's it! Oh, it's so good. Faster! I'll keep time with you! Whip his buttocks harder! Oh, he's swelling! I'm coming! Squeeze his balls, Ralph! Oh! Oh!' and heaving wildly, clutching the bedclothes with my hands, working my bottom as if dancing on a hot stove, my cunt, chock-full of that rigid robust mountain of hard flesh, I yelled with delight, frantically threw up my legs and, closing them around him, kicked his bottom with my heels, until he cried: 'Now it flies! Take that in your womb, and that, and that' – and the frantic Hercules forgetting all but that we were two animals in lecherous agony, yelled at me: 'You want fucking, do you; you want your belly full? Ain't you getting it? Take that! Suck every drop out with your puckering cunt, my pretty diddler!'

And I, wriggling, shrieking, and quivering with lust, called to him: 'Oh, it's heaven! My insides are flooded: I feel the sperm drops burn me as they hit my belly! I'm riddled with hot shots! Give me every charge in your gun! My buttocks are going and I can't stop. Whip him some more.'

For he had quieted his rapid motions. 'Yes!' he yelled. 'Flog me harder and I'll give her another dose without coming out?' 'You mean it?' I cried. For all

214

response he seized me in his arms lifted me up still spiked on his prick, and ran around the room with me; squeezing my backsides, putting his finger in my cul, thrusting his tongue in my mouth, and nibbling at my nipples while I sucked his tongue and clasped him tightly with arms and loins while Meg whipped both our bottoms until, at length, I again felt the thrill of his stiffening pego and, laying me again on the bed, he worked his heavenly probe in and out of my slit until I felt the great drops fly once again into me and with a shriek I fainted.

CHAPTER XIII

When I came to myself in bed in my darkened room, Ralph, all dressed, sat by my side while I clasped his neck in my arms.

'Madge, you are still young and new to voluptuous raptures. You've been going at it too hard. We have been selfish in spurring you on so fast. Gradually you will become hardened to amorous play and be able to bear all that we can give and take together. But now you need a rest and you must obey and leave that sensitive slit of yours alone for four days, or until Sunday. And, Madge, you mustn't excite John and I by going around with your lovely bubbies bare, or letting us see your lovely legs. It's pretty hard to swear off even for a few days. But, for the sake of your health, we must all sacrifice ourselves.'

I kissed the dear fellow and promised to obey him; so we passed three highly respectable days, walking, riding and avoiding all temptations until on Saturday night, I went to bed in perfect health and yearning eagerly to again feel that blissful balm in my belly.

When I awoke in the morning my thing quickly

216

reminded me that its itching was again to be solaced and, as I raised myself on my elbow, I gazed with gloating eyes down on that dear handsome lover of mine stretched out in bed on his back, still sleeping.

Gently I raised his nightshirt and feasted my eyes upon his innocent looking love shaft lying softly on the cushion-like testicles. Involuntarily my hand slid down over his belly and gently caressed the wrinkled weapon of lustful warfare.

Taking it in my fingers, with soft, quiet touches along its length, I saw, with flushing eyes and puckering slit, its softness swelled to stiffness, and soon my hand was filled with the rich rotundity of a glorious erection and my gloated eyes feasted on the round, red head, gorged with blood, and the gaping slit on its top, looking ready to spurt forth a shower of sperm.

Getting quickly onto my knees I drew my nightdress over my head and, without touching, straddled across him. Then, taking his prick in my hand, I held it bolt upright and, settling my body down upon it, it was soon piercing my vagina. In an instant a lustful, upward jerk of his buttocks made it disappear in my hole, and, glancing down, I saw that Ralph was awake and, with ardent gaze, watching my performances.

'Oh, you young lecherer! You couldn't wait until I woke up, but must ravish me in my sleep!' he laughed. 'You've kept me on short commons long enough,' I answered, 'and now I'm going to feast my belly full.' 'Well go ahead!' he cried, 'but you must do all the work yourself. Wait a second until I stuff this pillow under me; it will help give you a longer stroke.'

As I commenced to work my thighs with rapid,

ravishing heaves upon his stately prick, he cried out to me: 'Go to it, my pretty wench, my lovely, lusty lecherer, my sweet suction pump, my coral-cunted cock-pleaser, my dear whore, my ever ready sperm churner; wag your tail my lascivious little buttock worker! Push your slit tight on my belly, keep on – faster – faster!' Until, with a sudden spring forward he caught my bum in his hands and, with the burst of ultimate passion, threw me over on my back and, with straining muscles and bursting veins, gave me those sweet, final thrusts with such rapturous rapidity that my long stored juices oozed out around his pubes and wet his balls.

'I heard that hot-bellied cry way out in my room,' said a voice, and looking up, Uncle John stood by the bedside watching us with lustful eyes.

'She's got a fine action in her bum, John,' cried Ralph, 'let her pump up your sperm, herself.' And John, lying down with his buttocks on a settee, held his darling staff straight up in the air. Ralph lifted me astride of him while I put his cock where it would do the most good. I had just commenced working my thighs when Ralph, seeing a riding whip on the table, let it fall in tingling blows on my high lifted bottom until the excitement of the fight made his own cock get a hard-on and, tackling me behind, he stuck it in my cul while John was struggling to his feet. They both stood upright with me between them, lifted on their stiff staffs and having my whole body thrilled by their eager thrusts and copious shots of sperm.

As we rested and I lay there with two birds in my hand and sure of having them both in my bush, also,

'How shall we do it next?' I cried. 'Shall I tell you,' said John, 'how I first took a diddle?' 'That will be splendid!' I cried. And, settling ourselves in each other's way together, their hands gently caressing my slit and I holding in each hand the two pretty nightingales that had sung so often and so sweetly for me, he began.

CHAPTER XIV

'At sixteen I was a virgin. The sexual sensation had never been experienced and, if I had any amorous longings I did not know what they meant and my pintle was simply a piss-passer for me.

'One day I was climbing a smooth cherry tree, about as large around as Madge's waist, and, as I climbed up, with my arms and legs clasped tightly against it and rubbing up and down, my cock stiffened and a new sensation began to steal over me.

'Wondering what it was, I held the tree still tighter, instinctively, and worked my buttocks. Soon a delicious feeling spread all over me and centred itself in my prick, and as I kept on with faster heavings, I felt it stiffen in my breeches and soon it seemed to burst and shoot out something, I knew not what, while I felt that my belly was wet and a delightful languor spread over my whole body. I was astounded and clutched the tree until, too weak to hold on any longer, I slid to the ground. Lying there, I opened my breeches and found myself all covered with some sticky substance I had never seen before.

'I was half frightened, and went home and, stripping, washed myself and got on the bed, resolved to try if I could not recall those delicious feelings.

'As I took my cock in my hand and played with it I soon found that it grew bigger and bigger. It was soon stiff and swollen while the skin, which hid the head, soon yielded in a vigorous downward motion leaving the cap of love rosy and exposed.

'I did not know but what I had injured myself, but, spurred on by the exquisite pleasure I soon found my frigging hand made, I worked the skin up and down, faster and faster, and soon the same sensation which I had experienced on the tree stole over me. I felt something inside giving away and, in a delirium of delight, saw, for the first time, the milky seed fly high in the air and, keeping up the friction, squeezed out the last drop and lay back, panting.

'My eyes were half open. As I thought of this phenomena I wondered what it all meant until, one day, I saw our buxom servant girl leave the kitchen and, looking all around as if to see if she was watched, go into the barn.

'I followed, and, glueing my eyes to the wide crack in the boards, saw another crack that made my prick so stiff as to almost split my breeches open. The girl was in heat, had thrown herself, half reclining on her back, upon the hay full front to where I was peeping and had pulled her clothes up to her waist.

'I fastened my eyes on her broad hips and fleshy thighs, her fat, round belly heaving up and down, and the great mass of black, curly hair which was plainly in view between her outstretched thighs. Her face had an eager expression as she fixed her eyes upon her excited centre and, I quickly saw her hide it from view with her hand and, with extended fingers, rub herself up and down, seeming to penetrate into some opening there.

'Instinctively I tore open my trousers and, taking my cock in my hand, kept time with her self-deflowering motions until I heard her give forth a half-suppressed cry of satisfaction, heaving her hips more wildly and working her hand faster, spending, just as my own agile hand pumped out the white sperm that flew high up on the barn toward her.

'After that I kept my eye on her and, whenever I saw her go off by herself to the barn or bedroom, I quickly followed and gloating over the sight of her naked charms and lewd actions, joined her, unseen, in a revel of masturbation.

'In fact, I jerked myself off so often that I grew thin and weak and my father, not knowing the cause, wrote to a young curate whom he knew and sent me off to his distant parsonage for a change of air and to continue my studies under his care.

'The minister was an athletic young fellow of thirty and lived alone with his wife, a bright, pleasant faced, plump figured girl of twenty-two, overflowing with animal spirits and jolly, but proper and discreet, as became her position.

'For a week or so I left my cock alone. I was bashful, as I said, and the novelty of my surroundings kept me thinking of other things.

'But, passing her door one day, when she said she was going to take a bath. I couldn't resist peeping through the key-hole. There she stood, naked and lovely, sponging herself briskly with a towel; lifting one plump leg upon a chair, her naked, wide stretched thighs open to my eager eyes.

'I yielded to the fires that were burning within me and rushing to my room, ran to the open window and shot a full libation of sperm into the glistening sunlight.

'And I kept it up for a week until one day after dinner, when we were all in the library – the young dominie sat on the sofa and his wife on his lap – while I, opposite them at the window, pretended to be reading but was, in fact, furtively gazing with a carnal eye at the trim ankles and plump calves of his wife that her reclining attitude brought into view.

' "John," said the dominie, "I've got something to say to you. I know how I suffered at your age and I see you wrecking your health and want to save you." "What do you mean?" I asked. "You know what I mean," he answered kindly. And my flushed face answered him. "I've suspected that you were playing with yourself for some time, but yesterday, Molly here, saw you jerking yourself off in your room. Now, I've a proposition to make to you. If you will promise me on your honour, never to masturbate again while you are here – once a week, Molly will let you do anything you like with her. In plain English, today is Friday; every Friday you may fuck Molly to your heart's content, but for the rest of the week, you must leave lewdness entirely alone. Do you promise?" "Do you mean it?" I cried, jumping to my feet, my cock stiff in my breeches. "Doesn't this look like I meant

223

it?" he said, and seizing his blushing wife, he drew her across his lap as he lay extended on the sofa and, pulling up her clothes as high as they would go, exposed to my eyes her lovely body, naked from the waist down. "On your knees between her legs and swear to keep your promise," said the dominie. And kneeling there she seized my hand, pushed it down upon her lovely mount. "Kiss the book," she said. I was only a second there, for I was ready to spend, when rising to my feet, the lovely girl quickly unbuttoned my breeches and taking my over excited prick in her hand guided it quickly into her slit. "Fuck me!" she said. "Fuck me! I want it as much as you do!" And, eagerly grasping her bottom, I felt my pego pierce her tight crevice and enter her completely until belly touched belly and her hair curled in mine. I could not speak. I simply uttered an inarticulate cry of joy and commenced working in and out, as I had been taught by my frigging hand.

' "There! You naughty boy, isn't that nicer than playing with yourself?" And, throwing her arms around her husband's neck – "Are you jealous, hubby?" "Jealous?" he cried. "It's delicious! I enjoy the sight as much as you do the act. Give it to her, John!" "It's coming," I cried. "I am too," she answered. "Tickle the top of my slit, hubby." And the dear girl took my virgin offering deep into the recesses of her gaping womb.

'Then, reaching up she threw her arms around my neck and drew me down upon her, as we rained passionate kisses on each other. "Come!" cried the husband. "Let's have a Garden of Eden. Quick, run

224

to your rooms, strip and come back. Hurry up, see in what a state I am!" and he held up his big prick ready to burst.

'In two minutes there were two Adams and one Eve; and at once, Eve, making me lie on the sofa, threw herself across me and, taking the big pego of the original Adam, the handsome couple were soon pumping sperm at each other. Resting from their labours the lovely girl caught sight of my prick, which was sticking up stiff again. "See this wicked young cock, it is ready to crow again!"

'As I rolled off of her, her husband sprang forward. "By Priapus, Molly," he called, "now you have been taken in adultery you shall do what you have refused to do – suck my cock." "Yes, indeed, I will!" she cried. "Sit on the floor, then, between John's legs," he said, and her backsides were soon close to my belly while he, kneeling before her, stuck his great, inflamed cock invitingly into her face. Quickly her open lips closed over the ruby head and slid down the huge column, while one hand clutched his bum, and the other his testicles. "Work your lips just as you do your slit," he cried. What a luscious sight it was, but so short. "There it comes," and the swollen glands told that he was spending. Taking her hand away a minute, the sperm flew over her and over me, and then, seizing it again in her mouth, she did not let go until, with a deep sigh of satisfied emotion, he, himself, withdrew, melted by the fervour of her lips, tongue, and inhaling breath.'

CHAPTER XV

From the time when Ralph first rid me of my burden-
some and hateful maidenhead – carried it away on
the point of his lance – I had never so much as thought
of marriage. Our entwined arms and legs and his dear
shaft nailing me down to the couch of pleasure were
all the bonds I cared for. But, before long, he had to
return to New York. I hardly dared think of it; we
had been so full of the present, at least I had been so
full of their doings. One day I had been walking
alone and, returning, found Ralph and John talking
seriously. They seated me on the sofa between them
but didn't put their hands in my bosom or under my
skirts. I was really frightened; I thought that something had happened and looked anxiously from one
to the other.

'Madge, Ralph and I have been talking about the
future. I have business that will take me to the Pacific
in a few days and Ralph must return to New York
and you must go with him.' 'Oh!' I cried, 'I knew we
couldn't go on always as we are – but . . .' I got no

further, buried my face in my hands, and burst into tears.

To leave John was bitter, but since the night that he first possessed me, I had held Ralph in my heart, as so-called virtuous women do their husbands.

'Yes, Madge, Ralph and I have decided that you and he be legally married and go and live in New York.' 'Oh John, it's like taking half of my life away to leave you.' 'Of course, it seems so,' said Ralph, 'but John can visit us often, and we him.' And it was all settled.

One evening, not long after, I had gone to my room for something when Meg appeared, entirely naked, and said: 'Miss Madge, they want you in the parlour, in the same clothes I have on.' 'Oh Meg,' I said, 'I suppose they want us to take some of the starch out of them.' 'It's more than this, Miss.' And, curious, I stripped and followed her.

The room was brilliantly lighted. At the head of a couch in the centre, stood a priest, book in hand, while behind him, were Ralph, John and Sam, all three as bare as Meg and I.

I stood still with wonder; when John came forward and, leading me to the couch, threw me on my back. Then Ralph came forward and stood between my legs, his arrow aimed at my bull's-eye.

The priest stood at the side and, opening his book, commenced the short marriage service and, as he pronounced the declaration that we were man and wife, he took my hand and, making me grasp my newly-made husband's prick, guided it into my slit.

The dear fellow gave me a hard trot and, foundering at the end, invited John to follow him, which he did.

Then Ralph asked the priest to give me his blessing and the holy man, advancing to the altar, presented to our view a Priapus of immense size and got between my legs. 'Will you accept my blessing,' he asked, 'and let me anoint you with the holy oils?' 'Oh, Father, pour oil on my troubled waters.' And that stalwart prick of his went plunging into me and kept, pounding away until a profuse scattering of his sanctified sperm sent me off, wriggling, like a fish on a hook.

Then Ralph, turning to Sam, said: 'There is no black or white in heaven and her slit is at present heaven.' The well wound up and richly adorned fellow gave me a diddle that, for size of cock, vigour of action, and copious spending, was as perfect as the lovely grotto of Venus itself could have wished for.

CHAPTER XVI

And now the last night together came, and I suppose that you must anticipate a wholesale razzle-dazzle; but John and I felt the parting too keenly.

Ralph and I were in our room and I had just dropped my chemise and was sitting, naked, pulling off my stockings. 'Madge, go to John's bed and spend the night in his arms.' I kissed him fondly and went. Not forgetful of him, I ran to Meg's room, told her where I was going to pass the night and bade her go down to Ralph and see if he did not want to have a stroking match with her before he went to sleep.

Then I hastened to John, and entering the familiar room found it dark and he in bed. 'What's that?' 'Me, dear John; I've come to spend the night.' And, wrapped in his arms like a child in its father's, or a bride in her husband's, half tearful and half rapturous with our soft pleasures, I fell asleep on his breast.

Morning found us there, inhaling our souls into each other's lips, glued together, bellies throbbing and his dear shaft carrying soft rapture to my inner soul, until, in the ecstasy of our last embrace a knock came, and Sam entered with John's shaving water.

'Sam, you must say good-bye,' and soon his stalwart pego was buried within me and twice shot its elixer into my womb; the second time while I drew from John's dear staff the last libation of love.

Three hours later Ralph and I were on a train for the north.

The express was crowded, but finally the conductor came and told us a director of the road was occupying a state-room, and had consented to share it with us.

We found it a pretty apartment, shut from the rest of the car, with mirrors and carpets, easy chairs and an inviting looking sofa.

The occupant was a handsome man of fifty, and very courteous. 'I fear we shall disturb you,' said Ralph. 'No, I was getting lonesome and you are more than welcome to join me as far as Philadelphia where this car will be switched off.'

I threw myself on the sofa and watched the moving panorama as we passed the morning in pleasant talk. Once I caught my host's eyes, fixed with a gleam on my plump leg, which in changing position I had exposed.

When we stopped for dinner the two gentlemen alighted, brought me a lunch, and then promenaded the platform.

The train started again, when Ralph said: 'Madge, our host and I have been confidental; you ought to have heard the compliments he made of you! Go sit on his lap, and tell him he can have what he wants.'

'Stop your nonsense,' I said. But the laughing rascal took me in his arms and placed me in our host's lap.

'Won't you be kind to an amorous old codger and stay?' 'Yes, I will and I will make Ralph jealous!' I cried. And throwing my arms around my new lover's neck, I gave him a kiss.

I could feel his staff stiffen against my bottom and his hand instinctively pressed my breast. 'There, you naughty fellow! You shall have them at discretion,' and with both hands I lifted my plump titties out of my clothes and, with a cry of pleasure, he covered them with kisses.

'Pull up her petticoats and I will show you the way into her,' said Ralph, and, jumping up, he let loose his prick, fully recovered from Meg's drubbing.

'Bravo!' cried our host, and quickly snatching up all that hid my lovely legs, thighs and belly, as he called them, my bottom, was clasped in Ralph's hands and his staff was knocking at my slit.

'May I put it in?' said our host. 'Of course you may,' and he guided it in. 'You can squeeze his balls too, if you want to,' and he did. Seeing that we were spending he pushed his head down and with clinging lips and tongue, kissed and tickled my hot clitoris and Ralph's lunging shaft until, as it was withdrawn, the sperm still oozing from its gaping nozzle, he, unable to control himself, seized it in his mouth and sucked it. Fired by his emotions, he sprang to his feet, tore open his trousers and showed me a new morsel to be devoured by my hungry slit.

Ralph stretched me on my back on the floor, naked from the waist, and my grey-haired but virile

231

companion was in a moment a prisoner in my belly – a lively one, too – dancing like mad up and down, while I imprisoned his whole body with arms and legs until we both experienced the most delicious novelty of a first diddle between a congenial man and woman.

When we resumed the role of respectable members of society there wasn't a drop of love juice in either of them.

CHAPTER XVII

Reaching New York, we quickly settled down in the plain but cosy little flat that Ralph had, by writing, made ready for us.

A month passed in all the quiet pleasures of the usual newly married couple.

Then our first trouble came. We had spent all our money in fitting up our apartment and seeing the sights. John was too far away to help and we hated to borrow, and could only wait for Ralph's salary to come due.

Our landlord was a man – a muscular little hunchback of forty – who lived in bachelor quarters in the first flat.

He had been pleasant enough; but now, after calling two or three times for the money and receiving only excuses he began to grow angry and made us uncomfortable.

One morning, after Ralph had gone, a note was stuck under the door. He wrote that if he did not receive the rent that day we would have to move. I threw myself on the bed and burst into tears. Our cosy nest torn to pieces perhaps. Something must be done. Arranging myself, I decided to brave the little misformed lion in his den, all by myself.

Trembling, I knocked at his door. He called: 'Come in.' I found him writing at a table.

Standing opposite, I made my plea and begged him to wait a little longer and not break up our new home. The man was silent, but his bright, piercing eyes seemed to burn as they wandered over my person, which a chemise and a thin wrapper draped, but did not hide, the contour of.

He arose and, going to a window, gazed out with his back to me. Then he broke the silence. 'Madame, I am a man of business; debts are debts and must be paid. But I am also, a pleasure-seeker. If you are offended you can return to your room. Ever since you came into the house I have desired to possess you; watched you as you mounted the stairs, catching glimpses of your trim legs, and twice I have watched you and your husband, like youthful Venus and Mars, give your bodies up to each other's enjoyment, and causing my seed to be spilled on the ground. I am an ugly dwarf I know, more to be loathed than loved, but if you can forget your handsome lover and yield to my ardour, every outpouring will count to you a month's rent paid.'

'Never! I never sold myself, but – ' and I hesitated and threw myself into a great sleepy hollow chair. He stood facing me. 'But what?' 'If you love a man for love's sake, yea, for lust's sake – ' I did not finish, but, stretching out my legs as I reclined, I unbuttoned my wrapper and lay there, a tempting bit of fluff and fur from waist to heels.

'You splendid creature!' he cried, and, throwing himself on his knees between my thighs, kissed belly, legs and mount, but only for a second; then he jumped to his feet, stripped open his breeches and showed me the first circumcised cock I had ever seen. The great head was more freely exposed than a Christian's; it was of a length and thickness that recalled the immense erections of those black lovers of mine in the South.

'It's as big as you are!' I cried. Quickly aiming it at my excited target, he drove it in and, with athletic thrusts soon made me show, with wildly working belly, that I wasn't being fucked for cold cash, but was as eager as he was to exchange with him the white coinage of concupiscence.

'You're a very priestess of enjoyment,' he cried, and lifting me up in his strong arms he sat where I had been, and I lay straddled across him, his prick still in, his lips sucking my nipples. 'Oh,' I cried, 'that was delicious.' 'What would your husband say if he saw us here?'

'Do you think I would have let you, if he would object?'

And I told him how we were devoid of prejudices and each gladly yielded the mate to the lascivious pleasings of others.

'After my own heart! Why this clap-trap of fidelity, making necessity for brothels and adulteries leading oft to murder? Why shouldn't a man and woman who fancy each other shake cocks and cunts together as

235

well as hands? But come, my Venus, let me see you in true Venus costume.' And, devoured by his lustful gaze, I dropped the last veil and he likewise.

But he had heavy shoulders, muscular arms and legs, great, bulging buttocks – and, oh! – that cock, which was already recovering. Pressing me down upon the bed, he fixed his head between my thighs and, with admiring words and enlivening touches, examined the sheath of his pleasures. 'I too, like to know about the tools I use,' I said. He quickly knelt across my chest, and I fondled and caressed his enormous prick until he seized me and, with my weight, resting on my bubby cushions, my bottom raised, he standing behind me, grasped my hips in his hands and, gorged my slit with his giant erection. My body hanging there, as it were, on his firm pego, he swung me to and fro with ever increasing rapidity, my nipples titillated by friction against the bedclothes, until his balls, which knocked against my belly, gave up the fight and let loose their stores of satisfying sperm.

When I was rested I wanted to go back to my room. 'Not yet,' he said. And, as he sat on the edge of the bed, he put his head down to my thing and commenced tickling it with his tongue. His extended abdomen was asking my caresses and, bending over, I paid his kisses back to his cock which responded quickly to circling lips and titillating tongue.

'You naughty boy, you want me to eat it up.' 'Will you?' 'I'll do anything you want, and enjoy it as much as you do.'

He rolled over on his back, holding his prick and

said. 'Come.' 'I'll come, and you will too.' And, on my knees over his face, he seized my hips, raised his face to my quim, pressed the edges apart and darted his tongue within.

Rounding up my back so my mouth would reach his prick, and squeezing his balls, I took the red mouthful and sucked – and sucked – we both sucked, until the succulent glands gave up their stores and our breathless bodies lay panting in satisfaction.

CHAPTER XVIII

When I returned to my room I threw myself on the bed and dropped asleep. Waking late in the afternoon I had barely time to dress and get supper ready for Ralph. As I hurried around I noticed some papers stuck under the door and, picking them up, I found receipts for three months' rent; one for each fuck. Oh, how happy I felt. The crisis had passed and I could lift the care that was worrying Ralph.

It was Friday and I was determined to wait until Sunday before telling him. Worried, as he was, he did not touch me and I said to myself: 'Well my fine fellow, that's right, take a rest; store up a good stock of love cream in your testicles. You will want to flood me with it when I relieve your mind with my receipts.'

Sunday morning we lay in bed – just awake – and I turned to him, kissed him and passed my hand along his thighs till I felt his cock stiffening in my grasp. 'Come, Madge, I'm ashamed of myself for worrying so about this cursed rent. We'll forget it for today, at least, and have a good, old fashioned fuck.' And, sitting up in bed he pulled off his nightshirt and lying back, held up his stiffened staff ready to stick into me.

'Wait a moment!' and jumping up I ran naked in the closet, got the receipts, handed them to him and stood by the bedside, radiant. 'How did you get these?' he cried, and with a glib tongue I told him all. Then he seized me. 'You wicked little harlot, you make your room rent by renting your cunt to your landlord, do you?' And, flinging me on the bed he mounted me and plunging his cock full tilt into my ring of love, diddled me until we both lay panting happily.

I was describing my intrigue with the landlord when a knock interrupted me. Opening the door I found our landlord's card – and on the back written: 'Will you both join me for dinner, at one o'clock?' 'How nice,' I cried. 'You want to get that big prick of his in you again,' said Ralph. 'Of course I do,' I answered, 'and I bet you're dying to see that little dwarf put it in.' 'Right you are. But Madge, bathe this hard-on in cold water, I want to keep it for this afternoon.'

I obeyed, and succeeded in wilting it without losing anything. Then, dressing to avoid temptation, we went and breakfasted at a restaurant, and, taking a brisk walk, returned to the house feeling fine and ready to dine and diddle. We met our landlord at the door. 'I've told him all,' I said, and my tall hubby grasped the hands of the sturdy little new lover.

'Is the dinner to be a full dress affair?' I asked. They both laughed and Ralph answered: 'Let's wear nothing except stockings and nightshirts.' And, going to our rooms we soon looked like two angels ready to ascend, and I guess Ralph was, from the way he stuck out in front.

Slipping downstairs, when no one was around, we found our host ready. I must give him a name; let's call him 'Noah' – and laughing at our funny costumes we sat down, eating, drinking, and telling erotic episodes in our lives until the board lost its charm and we were eager for bed.

Raising his glass Noah said: 'I drink to the sweetest little cunt I ever tasted. May it always have what it wants as handy as now.' Laughing, I arose, slipping the disfiguring gown off my shoulders and standing there nude before them, one knee over the back of my chair – thus opening my slit wide – and, raising my glass: 'I drink to man, to the manliest part of him; and then those two dear images of Priapus so near to me. May they ever be ready, with rigid staff and juicy sperm, to carry rapture to any woman's cunt that is at hot as mine is now!' And I drained my glass to the bottom.

Both sprang to their feet, Noah on his chair, and dropping their shirts which hung a moment suspended on their pegos, they emptied their glasses and I was quickly in their arms.

A lascivious group of three, groping and frigging each other, soon stood beside the bed. 'After you,' said Noah to Ralph. With my dear hubby resting his shoulders on the edge of the bed, his feet on the ground, I straddled over him and could thus rape him standing upright.

'Let me put it in,' cried Noah, and, pointing the

dear yard straight up, I impaled myself on it and, grasping his buttocks in my hands: 'I'll ravish you!' I cried, and commenced to pump up his spermatic treasures with a lubric working bum, while the lustful Noah handled our battling organs and spurred us on with excited speech until my contracting cunny and Noah's frigging fingers drew from Ralph a belly full of seed. He did not wait to have his pego wilt inside of me, but pulled it out still rosy, rampant, and juicy, and drawing himself up flat on the bed, made me take his darling spending cock in my mouth. While from behind me on the floor, the immense pego of the excited clipyard was thrust into my suspended belly. I made my still lustful slit so tight and hard and deep that, when his mighty cock began to throb and spend, I had to let off my own excited emissions and return drop for drop, his vivifying emissions while my lips continued eagerly giving pleasure to Ralph's rosy rooster.

Lying throbbing on the bed they washed me off, gave me and themselves a reviving bumper of wine while Ralph, lighting a cigar, threw himself on a sofa and bade Noah do what he pleased with me. In two minutes his hands had groped and his lips had kissed every part of me and penetrated every cranny.

'What a delicious morsel of flesh she is!' he cried. 'What a delicious morsel of flesh this is!' I answered, caressing his stiffened shaft. 'It looks ready to inundate my womb again. 'It is!' he cried. And jumping up, my short but athletic lover seized me in his arms and standing bolt upright, putting his arms between my legs and grasping a cheek of my buttocks in each hand, he lifted me to a level with his face while I thrust my thighs around his neck, holding his head in my hands to steady myself. His nose just rubbing against my slit, his tongue penetrated it until I squirmed vigorously and he slid my body down along his chest till the stiff spear penetrated my gaping and excited slit. Calling to Ralph to whistle a jig, he danced briskly, while his swelling prick also danced lustfully to my insides and I kept time, with heaving belly and wriggling bottom until languor laid us on our backs on the bed.

'Your belly's too full for this,' said Ralph, kneeling over and holding up his prick in my face. I quickly devoured the tid-bit of raw flesh and washed the draughts of thick cream down with a plentious flow of saliva. 'Give me a taste,' excitedly exclaimed Noah; and, as I let myself fall back on the pillow the lecherous man with eager lips seized the full foaming spigot and sucked with eagerness the last sperm drops from Ralph's succulent prick.

'Are you disgusted?' asked Noah, as he drank a glass of wine. 'I haven't done such a thing in twenty years. Away back when I had the mining fever, we were snowed in one winter, six of us men, in one house way up in the mountains. We couldn't get out and time went slowly. One day, as we had just finished dining and each of us had three or four drinks of whisky in us, we discovered written in soot over the fireplace: 'Boys, let's suck each other's cocks.' We all looked at each other – who wrote it? All looked innocent when the rough but jolly leader spoke up: 'Boys I didn't write it but, damn it, it's set me thinking. I bet there is not a mother's son of you here who don't jerk himself off on the sly.'

'Then opening his breeches he pulled out his stiff prick. 'I'll suck any of you who will suck this.' Our pretended virtue melted away, and the rest of us eagerly produced our peckers. In a minute we divided into three couples and each of our mouths were full of fine erections and we were swallowing sperm at one end and spitting it at the other.'

This story, though vile according to our education, excited me and I threw myself between Noah's thighs and kissed his prick. Quickly grasping my buttocks he pulled them up to his head and plunging his tongue into my slit we both started on a sucking race, while Ralph, seizing a limber cane, tingled our heaving backsides with a rapid flogging.

CHAPTER XIX

The next morning when I got out of bed, long after Ralph had left, I found three letters under the door. The first was from Noah and contained a hundred dollar bill. 'Don't refuse this, dear girl, fifty thousand dollars wouldn't repay the pleasures I have tasted.'

The second was from my dear John and enclosed an introduction for Ralph to an old friend in New York. John wrote that his friend, Phillip Weston, was wealthy and might find Ralph more lucrative employment. Then he wrote tenderly and amorously about his thinking of me, and turning the page I read, 'Yes, my dear girl, as I sit here the thought of you sends a vigorous thrill through my shaft. I hold it in my hand wishing it in yours, or your plump bubbies, eager mouth, tight cul or sweet and luscious cunt. I lay it against the paper and trace it thus (here an outline of his prick) and now I fold the paper around it and frig into it the sperm your image raises.' All over the inside of the sheet were blotches of brown stuff that had been hot, rich cream, gushing from his dear pego. Opening my thighs I pressed the paper deep into my lustful crevice and, rubbing it and dreaming that his dear form was naked in my arms – I too, wet the paper and laid it aside to dry and send back to him.

The third letter was in a strange hand and, as I opened it, another hundred dollar bill dropped out. 'A slight memento my dear girl, of a delightful day in a parlour car.' No signature, but I knew that it was from that railroad director who let us into his private room and who I took into my private parts.

'Two hundred dollars,' I soliloquised, and, lifting up my thighs in the air I held them wide apart and gazed into the opening of my red crevice – 'Two hundred dollars just because you were nice to two men. Ah, if you were paid at that rate every time you sucked the delightful overflow out of your frisky guests, your owner would be a millionairess by this time.'

A key turned in the lock and Ralph entered. He burst out laughing. 'Don't stir, you're an awful smutty picture.' 'The picture is at your service,' I answered, hugging my legs closely down to the sides of my body, my feet at the side of my head. 'Keep that position,' he cried, pulling my wide-stretched buttocks to the edge of the bed and, placing my shoulders high on the pillows, devoured the lustful attitude for a minute. 'I'm going to suck you first, fuck you second, and then suck you again and, if you get out of that position before I get through, I won't diddle you for a week.' 'Hurry up then, I'm ready to spend now.' And his tongue was thrust into my cunt, stretched wider than ever before and brought down my ready juices almost immediately. 'Don't budge except to heave your ass,'

245

he cried out, into my still lustful slit he drove his excited penis, quickly sending the blissful balm to the inner parts to solace my lecherous agony, and, again on his knees, he kept his tongue working in my cunt and thrust a finger in my cul until I could stand it no longer and cried out that he would kill me if he kept on.

Then throwing himself on the bed, he made me fondle his prick and buttocks while he read the letters. Later, after a smoke with the landlord, he came up and said they were going to a theatre and, as I said good-bye to them at the door, the air seemed so fresh and invigorating that, though it was dark, I determined to take a walk.

Sauntering along looking into shop windows, I came into a side street which I afterwards found out was a cruising ground for women of pleasure. Presently a rough grasp on my shoulder startled me, and looking up, I saw it was a big, burly policeman. 'What are you cruising for, don't you get enough cocks staying in the house? Don't you know it's against the law?' I was too frightened to answer. 'By Jove, you're a new girl in these sections,' he continued, 'and a damned nice looking one. Come into the alley and let me see if the rest of you is as nice as your face.' And he dragged me along a dark narrow street. 'Please let me go!' I cried. 'You will either come with me or I will run you into the station,' he said. And, pulling me along the deserted alley we came to where a solitary lamp threw a flood of light down on a wagon. The powerful rascal seized me and threw me on my back on the tail board of a cart, my legs hanging down. 'Pull up your petticoats!' he ordered, 'I've no time to waste. The sergeant will be around shortly and will give me hell if he catches me off my post. See – I've got a good stiff-on.' And I saw his magnificent prick erect against his belly. It's the quickest way to get out of the scrape, I thought, and, pulling my clothes up to the pit of my stomach, I awaited his attack. 'Jolly, you're a daisy,' he said, passing his rough hand over thigh and belly and gave my brush a squeeze that made me wince.

'In it goes,' he cried. 'How's that for a stretcher?' I tried to keep still, but his big prick and splendid stroking made me forget all but the pleasure of his thrusts and I had to work my bottom. 'Oh, you like it, do you? You needn't deny it. I know when a girl shams and when she is tickled in the right spot.' And working harder, I gave myself up to it and cried out: 'It's lovely. Your splendid cock is making me spend.' 'So you shall, my dear,' and his colossal prick, knocking at my womb, shot its flood of lust into my cunt, sweltering in its own overflow.

'I've caught you, have I?' said a voice out of the shadow. 'Fucking a whore in the public streets and off your post.' And the speaker, another big policeman, stood looking down at our exposed lechery.

'Ah, now, Sergeant, what's the harm of diddling a gal? It don't take long. And Sergeant, look at her. She's a new one. See what a fine pair of legs and how her belly heaves; and her slit's as hot as a slut's. She gives a stroke up for every one down. Try her, Sergeant.' And, standing aside, he put his hands under my bottom and lifted me up to give his superior a better view of my venereal attractions.

The sergeant stepped between my legs. 'Well my dear, I don't want to be hard on your lover, so I'll be hard on you instead.' And, in an instant his splendid cock was plunged into me and another splendid diddle made me squirm. 'Meet us here again tomorrow night,' said the Sergeant, 'and don't come out of the alley till we are out of sight.'

When I did come out I was not long in getting home. I remember to this day the sensations of shame and fear I experienced that evening, but I also remember the uncontrollable pleasure those two police cocks, as big as their clubs, gave me on the wagon in the alley.

CHAPTER XX

It took me an hour to recover from the effects of the unexpected charge of the blue coated pair of lusty baton wielders. But I could not, despite the ignominy of having myself thus stormed and barbellied in the public street, be unconscious of the full fledged, firm fixed, fine fucking faculties of my last lovers. And my feverish, yes, ferocious fuck funnel forced me to feel the folly of feeling foolish over this fortuitous fornication, and set my brain to work to plan some new devilry; with my cunt as the centre of the celebration.

'I have it. I'll disguise myself and solicit Ralph and Noah on their way home.'

Donning some old clothes which I never wore, I again sallied forth at about the time the theatre was out and walked along the way I knew they would return.

I hadn't gone a block when two young fellows came along. 'Well sweetest,' said one, 'are you looking for a tenant, who'll move in your empty room, stay a while, dance a jig, and then vacate? By Jove, Jack.

She ain't bad. Damn the cost. Let's take her to Mother Jones' for a short razzle dazzle.'

'Go away and leave me alone!' I said. 'Leave you alone and unprotected? Oh, no,' said the youngster. 'Come along,' and each seized an arm. 'Where are you taking me?' I cried, 'To bed,' said one, and around a corner we went and up to a door. 'Here Mother, here's your dollar. Which room?' 'Is it for one jerk, or for the night?' said the buxom landlady. 'Oh, only a lightning thrust,' one answered. 'Then come into my room,' she said, and into a room we went. 'Pay her,' said the Madam, and the youngsters handed me a bill which I put into my pocket, and, in a jiffy, I was on the bed with a nice, young cock working in me. Then, fire, bang, and another was promenading in my Rue-Rogue. 'She'll do,' cried one. 'She's bully,' said the other. 'We'll make it longer next time.' And they were gone.

Fifteen minutes had hardly elapsed from start to finish. 'Well, my dear,' said the woman, 'that's quick work. If all your lovers take so little of your time you'll get rich quick. Clean up and take another stroll and you may land some more fish. The theatres are just letting out and I bet you will be back with a new stiff in an hour.'

I didn't answer. The word 'theatre' brought me back to what I had started for. So I left hastily to look for Ralph and Noah. Several men accosted me but I said that I was engaged.

Presently my old 'long and short of it' hove in sight. 'What a funny pair,' I said, laughing at their faces. 'You'll make fun of us, will you?' said Ralph, and he began groping me. 'There's nothing like novelty,' he continued, 'and my pego was stiff as soon as she hove in sight. Let's take her to your room for a brace of jerks. The other one will be asleep.'

So done, and into Noah's room we went, and when the gas was turned on there was a tableau. I took off my bonnet and they recognised me. I burst with a hearty laugh. 'I'll stop your laughing!' said Ralph, and, throwing me back on the sofa, he stuck his prick in my mouth for a stop cock, while my slit had another, of Noah's flesh.

One evening Ralph came home: 'Madge, I am going to leave for several days; not a word – I can't explain now. Noah will be your guardian meanwhile. Come help me pack.' As I packed I watched him bathe, till finishing he turned and said: 'Now for a farewell fuck.' In an instant I was on the bed with his dear form, almost in tears, but teeming with voluptuous rapture. Finished, he dressed and took me to Noah, and explained: 'Noah, you will play protector to her and see she doesn't want for anything. A field not ploughed and watered soon grows stale. Harrow her well; plough her frequently and irrigate her freely. I won't be jealous if you show her the lively sight of the city. Let her see and feel all she can, for it may be that my journey will result in our leaving New York and settling elsewhere.' He clasped me in his arms and was gone. The next day, Noah said that a Turkish bath would be the best thing to rejuvenate us and that he knew a quiet, small one where a man and a woman could take one together.

As he paid the female keeper he was asked which

rubber he wanted, and answered that he wanted the strongest.

Soon we were in a room as hot as my disposition, perspiring and naked, then sponged with cold water and plunged in a cool pool. I forgot all the processes which we went through alone. 'Now for the rubbing,' and entering the room, we found our manipulator awaiting us, a naked giant with a girdle around his loins. We had sheets thrown around us and Noah, dropping his, threw himself flat on a leather cot and the Negro commenced working his muscles, limbering his joints and rubbing him all over with the palms of his hands.

'Ah, Madge, that puts new life into me,' said Noah, as I watched the process. 'I should smile,' said the smiling rubber and he held up Noah's prick strutting perpendicularly. 'It feels as if he wanted something sweeter Miss.'

Throwing aside my sheet I told him to lift me up on top of Noah, and I was quickly taking the starch out of him. As I lay with his prick dissolved inside of me: 'Do you want to pump sperm into her?' asked Noah, 'let's see your cock,' and the lustful attendant stripped off the girdle and Noah and I had the brown and red sceptre in our grasp.

'Run,' said Noah, pushing me off the side. I ran around the room, the giant after me, until, rushing to Noah, he placed me on top of him; my belly over his face. As I took his prick in my mouth, the lustful black cock was guided by Noah into my slit and the God-like thrusts soon carried rapture through me and drowned my vitals in burning sperm while I gratified Noah with a hot-mouthed sucking.

Then we all took a plunge in the bath again and, coming out, 'Put the girdle on,' Noah said, 'so as not to tempt this young filly again.'

'No, no, I must have one more taste of this delicious prick,' and throwing myself on my knees before the giant, I caressed with hands, titties and mouth the already magnificent erection of his God-like cunt plough.

'You'll promise to quit with one more fuck?' 'I swear!' I cried. And, kneeling on the couch, Noah leaned my back against his breast, my bum on the edge of the bed. He bade the giant lift me up by the legs and, grasping them, he pulled them on each side of my shoulders, leaving my slit a gaping furnace with the doors wide open.

'What a fine view,' cried the Negro, dropping to his knees, and he not only viewed, but stuck his tongue into the stretched orifice. 'Stop, you'll make me spend,' I cried. 'So I will, Miss,' and, on his feet, he quickly drove his big prick to the hair in my cunt and fucked me until I squealed.

Two days later I was alone when a lady called. She was about my size and age; except she was a blonde and I was a brunette. She handed me a card – Mrs Philip Weston. 'Oh, yes, John had sent Ralph an introduction to Philip Weston – but we learned that he was away from the city.'

'Yes, your Uncle John wrote about you, but we have not been here since we received the letter.' She seated herself by my side: 'We'll be friends, shan't we?' I kissed her and she went on: 'Philip is away, but next week we sail south on our yacht. John, knowing that we're to be with him for a visit sent you this letter,' handing it to me.

'Dear Madge – It's no use. I can't live here without you and Ralph. I have written him to give up his position and for you and him to settle here with me, as the sole heirs of all I possess. You can come on with Mr and Mrs Weston.'

'Oh, how splendid,' I cried, gladly. 'And are you and John well acquainted?' I asked. 'That's a pointed question,' she laughed, 'but I know all about your relations with John and he knows as much about me as Philip does. We're both lewd, lustful women, and I'm not ashamed of it! Are you?' 'I live only for sexual enjoyment,' I answered.

'Let's strip and have our first embrace,' she cried. And soon a naked blonde and brunette were admiring, caressing, praising the charms of each other and, quickly on the bed, sought, with experienced tongues to quench the lustful fires that for the moment no man's pego was there to put out.

I told her of Noah – 'How funny to have a dwarf for a lover.' 'You'll have one in a minute.' I ran downstairs and, finding him, quickly told him, while I handled his prick: 'Strip here, clothes will only be in the way,' and in five minutes I introduced my lover to Mary.

Putting her on my lap, 'Come, Noah, and examine her,' and my dear lover was on his knees, kissing and tickling her swelling belly and luscious cunt, which she jutted out for him.

'Stop,' she cried, 'let me feel and kiss that big prick before you fuck me.' Kneeling over her, she soon had a mouth full of stiff prick and a handful of red balls.

'Quick, diddle me. I'm consumed with lechery,' she said, throwing herself back with extended thighs, and as he stuck his flaming nozzle to her door I guided it in.

How that woman loved it. How she heaved her belly, threw up her legs, pounded with her hands his bare bum, till on the verge of the precipice. 'Now, shoot it into me, I'm coming.' As I knelt beside the lustful warrior, the big prick swelled larger and larger. 'Ouch! there it comes. It's shooting all through me! Oh your lovely cock! Your delicious fucking! Give me every drop!' In a moment she lay heaving.

My cunt hot? I should say it was. I was flat on my back, my fingers clutching it. 'Stop! give her a taste of your tongue,' and Noah was in a moment sucking my slit, while she stuck her tongue in my mouth till I overflowed.

We did not separate till exhausted. Mary arranged to have me join her and Philip a week later in Philadelphia.

One evening Noah entertained three of his friends.

After they got lively he came and told me his friends were in a mood to appreciate a female friend, which he told them he would furnish if they would appear as Adam.

He led me naked into his room and introduced me

to three fine, stalwart clipyards. And, within fifteen minutes I had been well fucked by four cocks, and lay panting with the sperm oozing out of my slit.

Before Noah carried me to my room, twelve shots had been fired into my various holes.

CHAPTER XXI

All my attention was devoted to Noah the last week, and, when I said good-bye to him he talked more like a father than a lover, and gave me a certificate of deposit for two thousand dollars. 'Something for a rainy day,' he said.

Arriving at Philadelphia, I soon had Mary in my arms. 'Come to my room. For one night one room will do for the three of us, won't it?'

After a bath, she put her arms around me. 'Now dear, I'll introduce you to my husband.' Out from behind the window curtains stepped Philip Weston, stark naked, his rosy rooster ready to ravish me. Grabbing my arms she held them behind my back. 'Come examine this new cock cooler.' 'Cock cooler! The mere sight of it burns me up.' And, his hands and kisses covered me, then led me to the bed. His wife pointed his robust cock at my slit and, with a heave, he was in to the hilt.

The first fuck is always nice, and we played with agile loins until drained of our bliss. Two more

257

rounds, then, for the night he slept sandwiched between two warm specimens of woman flesh.

The next afternoon we boarded the yacht and were off for our long sail. The crew consisted of three big Italians and a Chinese cook who kept to the galley unless called for.

After land disappeared, Mary said: 'Come Madge, let's get into our high-sea rig.'

We were stripped to our stockings and were just reaching for our sailor suits when a voice from the doorway said, 'Missy, Captain Phil sent a bottle of wine.' 'Come in, Ah Wing,' and the cook entered in a blue blouse reaching to his knees, and served the wine as we lay stretched naked on the divan. 'Ah Wing, how's this for a pretty tickler?' as she raised one of my legs, showing my fucking facilities.

'Ah Wing, show the lady what a Chinese cock looks like,' and pulling his blouse over his head, stepped naked to the edge of the divan, and I had a Chinese prick in my hand for the first time. Long, and the end of it curved like a finger with the top joint bent, it was smaller around than a white man's, with a crisp little pair of balls, no bigger than a large dog's.

'Let Chinee-man kiss cunny,' and his tongue shot into my slit, when springing up: 'Me allee ready fuckee,' and I pointed his long, slim cock at my crevice and its curved end was soon tickling the instrument of joy. 'Ah, I see why you like the heathen fucking! Don't tickle the itching; Ah Wing will make me say ah-ah-ah in a second,' and he did.

Our sea clothes; our red jackets exposed our breasts at every flop, and a pair of pants in two pieces, only connected by the waistband, leaving our mounts exposed when we opened our legs, and when we stooped our bare bottom was exposed fully. 'Come on deck, I bet there is a quartet of stiff pricks ready to sing to us.'

All in line, with Phil in command, the four muscular men were stark naked, with stiff pricks, waiting for us.

'This is your initiation on board the *San Sousiand*, you must take the whole four of these shots into your pretty cunt,' and they threw me on one of the cushioned seats and, opening my legs, my belly and slit lay open to their lust.

I got soundly fucked by four pricks – one after the other, either of which would make a girl heave her belly, throw up her legs and spend! My cunt was as full as an ocean of water; I panted, writhed like a worm, and with glad ears drank in their words of appreciation as they shot into me their spermy fluid.

I lay, with legs fallen apart, panting breasts, heaving belly, and gaping slit; Mary hugging, kissing and congratulating me, until she saw the Chinaman leering at us from the galley. Springing up she rolled on her back at my side, opened wide her thighs and, that long slim cane was soon scratching the red and itching interior of her crevice.

A week of this; living around loose, and exchanging with each other every form of licentious lust – to describe it would be endless. I must turn to the last chapter, of our welcome at Beauvoir.

CHAPTER XXII

We sailed up the Mississippi to as near Beauvoir as we could, and Mary, Phil and I rode to the hermitage of my desires. Peeing through the window, we beheld John and Ralph reading in the library. I undressed entirely, then ran into the house and stood, eagerly happy, before my darling lovers.

Wild with delight and made to enjoy me, I denied them until, as naked as myself, first Ralph, then John, with firm, fierce, frenzied pricks, fucked me frantically.

I threw myself on their dear fallen spears and with lewd, loving lips and tongue, brought them to life again. Then Mary and Phil came bounding through the window, where they had watched the first shots fired, and faced us, naked.

'Now I'll introduce you to my husband, as you did to yours,' and guiding Ralph's prick into her, we watched these lusty lovers taste for the first time the sweets of cock and cunt.

Then, John quickly sprang into her saddle and her husband into mine and our jockeys, riding gallantly, our bellys were soon inundated at the first finish of frenzied fucking.

Glancing through the window I spied Sam. I darted out and threw myself in his arms. 'Strip, quick, and carry me into the house on your prick.' And, in a minute, his staff was deep in my belly and, running full tilt, he entered the house and fucked me before the whole company. I squirmed off my still stuck up slit-sticker and, turning it to Mary's face: 'Kiss it – suck it – make it firm again, so he can give your slit a creamy womb opener.'

With her labial touches, his prick with stiffened, swelling glands filled her mouth and, grabbing her, he threw her on her back and fucked her into a spasm of spending.

In the doorway appeared my darling Meg, and I led her in, and tearing off her clothes, I turned to Phil: 'Isn't she pretty? Brown Venus!' 'Splendid!' and quickly his hands and lips fired at her every touch. 'My slit's on fire – seething,' she cried, and on the couch he gave her a fervent fuck.

We supped naked, each of us drinking a full bottle of champagne. In a dancing, prancing, devil-may-care stage of intoxication, we seven naked, in a group of writhing bodies close together, staggered and reeled into the parlour. And all in a bunch, topsy-turvy, kneeling, lying down, cocks in cunts, in culs, in titties, mouths and hands, we went off together and were flooded, inside and out, with showers of sperm, faces and forms glistening with the shiny emissions and cocks, cunts and mouths covered with the exuberant overflow.

I was too far gone to watch the others. I know that one of the fellows' whiskered mouths was kissing my bottom, thighs and belly and opening my slit. A languid tongue was licking the ruby interior while a fallen prick was six inches from my face. I took it in my mouth and rolled my tongue over it, pulling the hair with my teeth and, taking the crumpled skin in my mouth feasted upon the pearly drops that still oozed from it. John attempted to go out to make water, but Mary took his flabby prick in her mouth and, I could see by the motions of her throat she was swallowing his come. Strangling, she jumped up, shouting, 'Oh, it makes me want to come, too.' John putting his head in her slit cried, 'Come, then!'

Jumping to his feet he seized the shameless Mary, holding the big thighs wide open and, putting her cunt on Sam's big prick, wrapped her legs around his waist. Pushing his cock out for me to wet, he took it out of my mouth and pointed it at Mary's bum, entered it, and the delighted girl screamed with pleasure. Fucking briskly, each cock plunged in and out at the same time, then giving out screams of overwrought excitement, she received the streams from both cocks. And, as her stallions fell exhausted on the floor, she threw herself on top of them and seemed to be eating up their fallen pricks.

The other two men rushed to me and, one in my cunt and one in my mouth, flooded me with sperm and rapture.

Sam, stooping down, put his arms between our legs and, lifting us up, forked thus, and off with us to our

room, where he bathed us, laid us in bed as each-
pressed a good-night kiss on his pego and he on our
slits.

CHAPTER XXIII

But, dear Jack, I must stop somewhere, and it shall be with this chapter.

The men arranged a fishing trip and we, poor girls, were left vacant. While lamenting our luck, I heard the gate open, and looking out saw the priest who had married us, coming up the walk.

Laying Mary flat on her back on the sofa I opened the front of her dress to expose her bubbies and, raising one knee, pulled her skirts up so that, by stooping, he could get a full view of her coral cavity. Then I hid myself behind a curtain.

When no one responded to his knock he walked to the piazza and finding the shutters were opened he walked in.

Mary's form caught his eye and in a minute he was kneeling at her side: 'Holy Virgin, what a pretty prick pleaser,' he muttered, but as he looked closer, 'That isn't the girl I fucked on her wedding night: it might be the other fellow's wife.' He gently lifted her skirts, and, as if moving in her sleep, she let her legs drop wide open and he had the whole kingdom of heaven exposed to him. Jumping up he took out his monster, then knelt between her legs, lifting them up, the true cross which women love to bear was quickly stored away in her innermost sanctuary.

'Oh, I can't play asleep!' cried Mary. 'It's too heavenly! Fuck harder if you'd save me from eternal regrets. Come, Madge, and see this royal priest's relic giving my cunt a sample of the church's creamy charity. As fast as you like, father, I'm ready.'

As I watched the charming cunt and colossal cock charging at each other with such rapidity, I grew dizzy and fell back on the floor.

In a minute the priest's sperm-spouting prick was relieving me of my rich store of oily oblation as Mary knelt beside us and squeezed the balm out of his buttocks.

He did not leave us till all our holes had hotly held his fresh and fecundatious prick. When he left, a pecker pronely pulseless, or testicles more wholly empty, could not be found in the buttock wagging world.

Walking along the brook the next day, we heard, 'Mine's bigger than yours – I bet I can shoot it further than you!' and we looked down on two lads finishing their bath, and playing with their stiff cocks.

'They'll waste it if we don't hurry,' said Mary. 'You naughty boys, aren't you ashamed to play with those things! They don't belong to you at all, but are for the girls.' And pulling me beside her, she dragged my skirts to my waist, and I did the same to her. We soon had their pretty pricks plugging us to the delight

265

of the four. Then we let them examine us and they were soon again deep in our slits.

When we continued our walk we came upon a black man slouching along. He stood still and I saw his lustful eyes on our trim figures, and I knew he was thinking how easy it would be to rape us both.

I walked up to him. 'Do you remember me?' He looked doubtful. 'I've seen you, Miss, but ain't placed you.' Then – 'Hell,' he cried. 'This tells me,' and he pulled out his monstrous cock. 'I fucked you a year ago.' And in two minutes I was fucked again.

'Oh,' cried Mary, 'help' and she grasped her burning slit. But the man, grabbing one of us in each arm, carried us, running to his hut and threw us on the same grassy mound my rump had pressed a year before.

Another black man, naked, appeared at the door. 'Hurry, Bob. I've fucked one and the other wants it bad!' And, as the lust-burned girl opened her legs, the twin of the last erection was plunged, and lunged into a hole hot enough to turn an anchorite into a satyr. And, the dancing belly received a load that made her feel that heaven and earth were in conjunction on the fiery bed of hell. We stripped bare, and I threw the hot bellied girl again on her back and put her lover's prick into her slit. I then knelt with my gaping grotto over her face, and with her late gizzard tickler plunged into it, I felt her licking my well-filled cunt and my stallion's flying shaft, till as he was spending I jerked it out and stuck it in her face, watching her with one giant in her cunt and a sperming spigot in her eager mouth.

One of the men threw himself on the girl, pierced her with his rampant prick, then rolled over on the ground, finally stopped with Mary on top, till, with a lustful cry she sprang up and squatted over his mouth, and seized his fallen monarch reeking with albumen in her mouth.

The other fellow picked me up and, belly to belly started running, forcing his prick in me as we went, and fucked me on the fly until we spent. Then he dropped me on my elbows, seized my legs and spiked as I was turned completely over and continued to fuck me till, exhausted, he fell beside me and licked my lust laden slit as I sucked his giant prick.

Enough! Dear Captain Jack! If this works on you as it does on me, all the squaws on the plains will be giving birth to Little Jack Gardners, Jr.

Still with the bunch; when your next furlough comes we will welcome you.

I will not justify myself for writing frankly, for my voluptuous soul snaps its fingers in the face of respectability.

I am made of flesh and blood, and all it can accomplish, on pleasure bent, I would experience.

Pucker, poor prude! Pinch yourself in the dark, under the bed clothes, run away from a man in his shirt-sleeves – but for me – give him to me flesh to flesh, lips to lips, breast to breast, belly to belly, and his bold, blissful cock carrying rapture to my ever yearning cunt – I live for lust alone!

HELP US TO PLAN THE FUTURE OF EROTIC FICTION –

– and no stamp required!

The Nexus Library is Britain's largest and fastest-growing collection of erotic fiction. We'd like your help to make it even bigger and better.

Like many of our books, the questionnaire below is completely anonymous, so don't feel shy about telling us what you really think. We want to know what kind of people our readers are – we want to know what you like about Nexus books, what you dislike, and what changes you'd like to see.

Just answer the questions on the following pages in the spaces provided; if more than one person would like to take part, please feel free to photocopy the questionnaire. Then tear the pages from the book and send them in an envelope to the address at the end of the questionnaire. No stamp is required.

THE NEXUS QUESTIONNAIRE

SECTION ONE: ABOUT YOU

1.1   Sex *(yes, of course, but try to be serious for just a moment)*
      Male ☐   Female ☐

1.2   Age
      under 21 ☐   21 – 30 ☐
      31 – 40 ☐   41 – 50 ☐
      51 – 60 ☐   over 60 ☐

1.3   At what age did you leave full-time education?
      still in education ☐   16 or younger ☐
      17 – 19 ☐   20 or older ☐

1.4   Occupation _____

1.5   Annual household income
      under £10,000 ☐   £10–£20,000 ☐
      £20–£30,000 ☐   £30–£40,000 ☐
      over £40,000 ☐

1.6 Where do you live?
     *Please write in the county in which you live (for example
     Hampshire), or the city if you live in a large metropolitan
     area (for example Manchester)* _____

SECTION TWO : ABOUT BUYING NEXUS BOOKS

2.1 How did you acquire this book?
     I bought it myself ☐   My partner bought it ☐
     I borrowed it / found it ☐

2.2 If this book was bought ...
     ... in which town or city?   _____
     ... in what sort of shop: High Street bookshop ☐
                                   local newsagent ☐
                                   at a railway station ☐
                                   at an airport ☐
                                   at motorway services ☐
                           other: _____

2.3 Have you ever had difficulty finding Nexus books on sale?
     Yes ☐   No ☐
     If you have had difficulty in buying Nexus books, where
     would you like to be able to buy them?
     ... in which town or city   _____
     ... in what sort of shop from
         list in previous question _____

2.4 Have you ever been reluctant to buy a Nexus book because
     of the sexual nature of the cover picture?
     Yes ☐   No ☐

2.5 Please tick which of the following statements you agree with:
     I find some Nexus cover pictures offensive/
     too blatant ☐

     I would be less embarassed about buying Nexus
     books if the cover pictures were less blatant ☐

     I think that in general the pictures on Nexus books
     are about right ☐

     I think Nexus cover pictures should be as sexy
     as possible ☐

SECTION THREE: ABOUT NEXUS BOOKS

3.1   How many Nexus books do you own? _____

3.2   Roughly how many Nexus books have you read? _____

3.3   What are your three favourite Nexus books?
      First choice   _____
      Second Choice   _____
      Third Choice   _____

3.4   What are your three favourite Nexus cover pictures?
      First choice   _____
      Second choice   _____
      Third choice   _____

SECTION FOUR: ABOUT YOUR IDEAL EROTIC NOVEL

We want to publish books you want to read – so this is your chance
to tell us exactly what your ideal erotic novel would be like.

4.1   Using a scale of 1 to 5 (1 = no interest at all, 5 = your
      ideal), please rate the following possible settings for an
      erotic novel:
      Medieval/barbarian/sword 'n' sorcery   ☐
      Renaissance/Elizabethan/Restoration   ☐
      Victorian/Edwardian   ☐
      1920s & 1930s – the Jazz Age   ☐
      Present day   ☐
      Future/Science Fiction   ☐

4.2   Using the same scale of 1 to 5, please rate the following
      styles in which an erotic novel could be written:
      Realistic, down to earth, set in real life   ☐
      Escapist fantasy, but just about believable   ☐
      Completely unreal, impressionistic, dreamlike ☐

4.3   Would you prefer your ideal erotic novel to be written from
      the viewpoint of the main male characters or the main
      female characters?
      Male   ☐   Female   ☐

4.4   Is there one particular setting or subject matter that your
      ideal erotic novel would contain?
      _____

SECTION FIVE: LAST WORDS

5.1 What do you like best about Nexus books?

_____

_____

5.2 What do you most dislike about Nexus books?

_____

_____

5.3 In what way, if any, would you like to change Nexus covers?

_____

_____

5.4 Here's a space for any other comments:

_____

_____

_____

_____

_____

_____

_____

_____

_____

Thank you for completing this questionnaire. Now tear it out of the book – carefully! – put it in an envelope and send it to:

Nexus Books
FREEPOST
London
W10 5BR

No stamp is required.